THE ITALIAN'S CHRISTMAS HOUSEKEEPER

SHARON KENDRICK

MILLS & BOON

First Published in Great Britain 2018
by Mills & Boon, an imprint of HarperCollins*Publishers*
1 London Bridge Street, London, SE1 9GF

© 2018 Sharon Kendrick

ISBN: 978-0-263-07712-4

MIX
Paper from
responsible sources
FSC C007454

This book is produced from independently certified FSC™ paper
to ensure responsible forest management.
For more information visit www.harpercollins.co.uk/green.

Printed and bound in Great Britain
by CPI Group (UK) Ltd, Croydon, CR0 4YY

To Maura Sabatino, who is funny and beautiful
and whose help for this book was invaluable.

Grazie mille for bringing Naples alive with
your words—and for helping me to
create a Neapolitan Christmas!

CHAPTER ONE

SALVIO DE GENNARO stared at the lights as he rounded the headland. Flickering lights from the tall candles which gleamed in the window of the big old house. They made him think of Christmas and he didn't want to think about it—not with still six weeks left to go. Yet here in England the shops were already full with trees and tinsel and the kind of gifts surely no sane person would want for themselves.

His mouth hardened as the dark waters of the Atlantic crashed dangerously on the rocks beneath him.

Christmas. The *least* wonderful time of the year in his opinion. No contest.

He slowed his pace to a steady jog as dusk fell around him like a misty grey curtain. The rain was heavier now and large drops of water had started to lash against his body but he was oblivious to them, even though his bare legs were spattered with mud and his muscles were hot with the strain of exertion. He ran because he had to. Because he'd been taught to. Tough, physical exercise woven into the fabric of his day, no matter where in the world he was. A discipline which was as much a part of him as breathing and which made him hard and strong. He barely noticed that his wet singlet was now clinging to his torso or that his shorts were plastered to his rocky thighs.

He thought about the evening ahead and, not for the first time, wondered why he had bothered coming. He was here because he wanted to buy a prime piece of land from his aristocratic host and was convinced the deal could be concluded more quickly in an informal setting. The man he was dealing with was notoriously difficult to pin down—a fact which Salvio's assistant had remarked on, when she'd enquired whether she should accept the surprise invitation for dinner and an overnight stay.

Salvio gave a grim smile. Perhaps he should have been grateful to have been granted access to Lord Avery's magnificent Cornish house, which stood overlooking the fierce midwinter lash of the ocean. But gratitude was a quality which didn't come easily to him, despite his huge wealth and all the luxury it afforded him. He wasn't particularly looking forward to dinner tonight. Not with a hostess who'd been eying him up from the moment he'd arrived—her eyes lit with a predatory hunger which was by no means unusual, although it was an attitude he inevitably found tedious. Married women intent on seduction could be curiously unattractive, he thought disdainfully.

Inhaling a lungful of sea air, he grew closer to the house, reminding himself to instruct his assistant to add a couple of names to the guest list for his annual Christmas party in the Cotswolds, the count-down to which had already begun. He sighed. His yearly holiday celebration—which always took place in his honeystone manor house—was one of the most lusted-after invitations on the social calendar, though he would have happily avoided it, given the opportunity. But he owed plenty of people hospitality and you couldn't avoid Christmas, no matter how much the idea appealed.

He'd learnt to tolerate the festival and conceal his aversion behind a lavish display of generosity. He bought expensive gifts for his family and staff and injected yet more cash into the charitable arm of his vast property empire. He took a trip to his native Naples to visit his family, because that was what every good Neapolitan boy did, no matter how old or successful he was. He went back to the city which he avoided as much as possible because it was the home of his shattered dreams—and who liked to be reminded of those? For him, home would always be the place where he had been broken—and the man who had emerged from the debris of that time had been a different man. A man whose heart had been wiped clean of emotion. A man who was thankfully no longer at the mercy of his feelings.

He increased his pace to a last-minute sprint as he thought about Naples and the inevitable litany of questions about why he hadn't brought home a nice girl to marry, nor produced a clutch of bonny, black-haired babies for his mother to make a fuss of. He would be forced to meet the wistful question in her eyes and bite back the disclosure that he never intended to marry. *Never.* Why disillusion her?

He slowed his pace as he reached the huge house,

glad he had declined his hostess's invitation to accompany her and her husband to the local village that afternoon, where a performance of Cinderella was taking place. Salvio's lips curved into a cynical smile. Amateur dramatics in the company of a married woman with the hots for him? Not in this lifetime. Instead, he intending making the most of the unexpected respite by trying to relax. He would grab a glass of water and go to his room. Listen to the soothing soundtrack of the ocean lashing hard against the rocks and maybe read a book. More likely still, he would chase up that elusive site in New Mexico which he was itching to develop.

But first he needed to dry off.

Sinking her teeth into a large and very moist slice of chocolate cake, Molly gave a small moan of pleasure as she got her first hit from the sugary treat. She was starving. Absolutely starving. She hadn't eaten a thing since that bowl of porridge she'd grabbed on the run first thing. Unfortunately the porridge had been lumpy and disappointing, mainly because the unpredictable oven had started playing up halfway through making it. Not for the first time, she wondered why her bosses couldn't just have the kind of oven you simply switched on, instead of a great beast of a thing which lurked in the corner like a brooding animal and was always going wrong. She'd been working like crazy all morning, cleaning the house with even more vigour than usual because Lady Avery had been in such a state about their overnight guest.

'He's Italian,' her employer had bit out. 'And you know how fussy they are about cleanliness.'

Molly didn't know, actually. But more worrying still was Lady Avery's inference that she wasn't working hard enough. Which was why Molly dusted the chandeliers with extra care and fastidiously vacuumed behind the heavy pieces of antique furniture. At one point she even got down on her hands and knees to scrub the back door porch—even if she did manage to make her hands red raw in the process. She'd put a big copper vase of scented eucalyptus and dark roses in the guest bedroom and had been baking biscuits and cakes all morning, so that the house smelt all homely and fragrant.

The Averys rarely used their Cornish house—which was one of the reasons why Molly considered being their resident housekeeper the perfect job. It meant she could live on a limited budget and use the lion's share of her wages to pay off her brother's debt and the frightening amount of interest it seemed to accrue. It was the reason she endured the isolated location and demanding attitude of her employer, instead of spreading her wings and finding somewhere more lively.

But the winter had made her isolation all the more noticeable and it was funny how the approach of Christmas always reminded you of the things you didn't have. This year she was really missing her brother and trying not to worry about what he was doing in Australia. But deep down she knew she had to let go. She *had* to. For both their sakes. Robbie was probably having the time of his life on that great big sunny continent—and maybe she should count her blessings.

She took another bite of chocolate cake and did exactly that, reminding herself that most people would revel in the fact that when the Averys *were* around, they entertained all kinds of amazing people. Guests Molly actually got to meet—even if it was only in the context of turning down their beds at night or offering them a home-made scone. Politicians who worked with Lord Avery in the Palace of Westminster, and famous actors who spouted Shakespearean sonnets from the stages of London's theatres. There were business people, too—and sometimes even members of the royal family, whose bodyguards lurked around the kitchen and kept asking for cups of tea.

But Molly had never heard Lady Avery make such a fuss about anyone as she'd done about the impending arrival of Salvio De Gennaro, who was apparently some hotshot property developer who lived mostly in London. Earlier that day she had been summoned into her boss's office, where the walls were decked with misty photos of Lady Avery wearing pearls and a dreamy expression, in those far-off days before she'd decided to have a load of extensive work done on her face. A bad idea, in Molly's opinion—though of course she would never have said so. Lady Avery's plump lips had been coated in a startling shade of pink and her expression had been unnaturally smooth as she'd gazed at Molly. Only the hectic flicker in her pale eyes had hinted how excited she was by the impending visit of the Italian tycoon.

'Everything is prepared for our guest's arrival?' The words were clipped out like tiny beads of crystal.

'Yes, Lady Avery.'

'Make sure that Signor De Gennaro's bed linen is scented with lavender, will you?' continued her boss. 'And be sure to use the monogrammed sheets.'

'Yes, Lady Avery.'

'In fact...' A thoughtful pause had followed. 'Perhaps you'd better go into town and buy a new duvet.'

'What, *now*, Your Ladyship?'

'Yes. Right now.' A varnished scarlet fingernail began tracing a circle on the sheet of blotting paper on the desk and an odd, trembling note had crept into her employer's aristocratic voice. 'We don't want Signor De Gennaro complaining about the cold, do we?'

'We certainly don't, Lady Avery.'

The last-minute purchase of the new duvet had been the reason why Molly hadn't been on hand to greet the Italian tycoon when he'd arrived. And when she'd returned from her shopping expedition—gasping under the bulky dimensions of a high-tog goose-down duvet—there had been no sign of him. Only his open suitcase and a few clothes strewn around his room indicated he was somewhere in the vicinity, although he was nowhere to be seen in the house. Which at least meant Molly had been able to make up his bed in peace—though her heart had started racing when she'd spotted the faded denims slung carelessly over a stool. And when she'd picked up the dark sweater which lay crumpled beside it, she had been startled by the softness of the cashmere as she'd automatically started to fold it. Briefly, her fingertips had caressed the fine wool before she had taken herself downstairs for tea and some restorative cake and she was just on her third mouthful when the kitchen door opened then slammed shut with a rush of icy air and Molly looked up to see a man framed in the doorway who could only be the Italian billionaire.

Her heart crashed against her ribcage.

The most perfect man she could have imagined.

Her mouth opened slightly but she clamped it shut and the chocolate fudge cake she'd been eating suddenly tasted like glue against the roof of her mouth.

Mud-spattered and windswept, he was standing perfectly still—his singlet and shorts surely the craziest choice of clothes he could have selected for the bitter winter day, although a fleecy top was knotted around his narrow hips. His olive skin was silky-smooth and his body was... Molly tried not to shake her head in disbelief but it took some doing, because his body was sensational—and she was certainly not the kind of woman who spent her time analysing men's bodies. In fact, her interest had never really been sparked by anyone.

Until now.

She swallowed, the cake she was holding suddenly forgotten. It took a lot for Molly to disregard the sugar craving which had always been the bane of her life, but she forgot it now. Because she'd never seen a man like this. Not someone with a rocky torso against which his wet top clung to every sinew, as if it had been painted on with a fine-tipped brush. Nor such narrow hips and sculpted thighs whose glorious flesh was exposed by the shorts he seemed to wear so comfortably. Her eyes moved up to his face. To eyes as black as one of those moonless nights when you couldn't ever imagine seeing daylight again. And his lips. Molly swallowed again.

Oh, those lips. Sensual and full, they were hard and un-smiling as they looked at her with something it took a moment for her to recognise. Was it...*disdain*? Her heart pounded uncomfortably. Yes, of course it was. Men with whiplike bodies which didn't carry an ounce of extra weight would be unlikely to approve of an overabundant female who was bulging out of her ugly uniform and stuffing a great big fix of carbohydrate into her mouth.

Flushing to the roots of her hair, she put down the half-eaten cake and rose to her feet, wondering why the ground beneath them suddenly felt as if it were shifting, the way she'd always imagined standing on quicksand might feel. 'I'm...' She blinked at him before trying again. 'I'm so sorry. I wasn't expecting anyone...'

His voice was sardonic as his gaze met hers for one heart-stopping moment, before dropping briefly to the crumb-laden plate. 'Clearly not.'

'You must be...' *A dark angel who has suddenly fallen into my kitchen? The most gorgeous man I've ever seen?* Her chest felt tight. 'You must be Signor De Gennaro?'

'Indeed I am. Forgive me.' Jet eyebrows were raised as he unknotted the warm top from his hips and pulled it over his head before shaking out his damp, dark curls. 'I seem to have disturbed your snack.'

Her *snack*? Although his English was faultless, his richly accented voice was nearly as distracting as his body and Molly opened her mouth to say it was actu-ally a late lunch because she'd been rushing around all morning preparing for *his* arrival, but something stopped her. As if someone like Salvio De Gennaro

would be interested in her defence! As if he would believe her making out she was a stranger to cake when
her curvy body told an entirely different story. Smoothing her uniform down over her generous hips, she tried
to adopt an expression of professional interest, rather
than the shame of being caught out doing something
she shouldn't. And he was still staring at her. Making
her aware of every pulsing atom of her body in a way
which was making her feel extremely self-conscious…
but strangely enough, in a *good* way.

'Can I get you anything, Signor De Gennaro?' she
questioned politely. 'I'm afraid Lord and Lady Avery
have gone to the village pantomime and won't be back
until later.'

'I know,' he said coolly. 'Perhaps some water. And
a coffee, if you have one.'

'Of course. How do you take your coffee?'

He flickered her a smile. 'Black, short, no sugar.
Grazie.'

Of course not, thought Molly. No sugar for someone
like him. He looked as if he'd never been near anything
sweet in his life. She wished he'd go. Before he noticed
that her brow had grown clammy, or that her nipples
had started to push distractingly against the unflatter-
ing navy-blue uniform Lady Avery insisted she wore.
'I'll do that right away,' she said briskly. 'And bring
them up to your room.'

'No need for that. I'll wait here,' he said.

She wanted to tell him he was making her feel awkward by standing there, like some kind of brooding,
dark statue—just *staring* at her. As if he had read her

thoughts, he strolled over towards the window and she became aware of an almost imperceptible limp in his right leg. Had he injured himself when out running and should she ask him whether he needed a bandage or something? Perhaps not. Someone with his confidence would be bound to ask for one.

She could feel a stray strand of hair tickling the back of her neck and wished she'd had time to fix it. Or had been sitting reading some novel which might have made her look interesting, instead of scoffing cake and emphasising the fact that she was heavy and ungainly.

'I'll try to be as quick as I can,' she said, reaching up into one of the cupboards for a clean glass.

'I'm in no hurry,' he said lazily.

Because that much was true. Salvio had decided that he was enjoying himself though he wasn't quite sure why. Maybe it was the novelty factor of being with the kind of woman he didn't come across very often—at least, not any more. Not since he'd left behind the back-streets of Naples, along with those women whose curves defined fecundity and into whose generous flesh a man could sink after a long, hard day. Women like this one, who blushed alluringly if they caught you looking at them.

He had waited for a moment to see if she would recognise him. If she knew who he was—or, rather, who he *had* been. But no. He was familiar with recognition in all its forms—from greedy delight right through to feigned ignorance—but there had been no trace of any of those on her face. And why should there be? She was much younger than him and from a different country.

How would she have known that in his native Italy he had once been famous?

He watched her busying herself, her curvy silhouette reminding him of the bottles of Verdicchio which used to line the shelves of the city bar he'd swept as a boy, before the talent scouts had discovered him and ended his childhood. She turned to switch on the coffee maker and a sudden dryness turned his throat to dust because...her breasts. He swallowed. *Madonna mia*—what breasts! He was glad when she turned away to open the fridge door because his erection was pressing uncomfortably against his shorts, though, when she did, he then became mesmerised by her shapely bottom. He was just fantasising about what her shiny brown hair would look like loose when she turned around and surveyed him with eyes as grey as the Santissima Annunziata Maggiore—that beautiful church in Naples, which had once been an orphanage.

Their gazes clashed and mingled and something unspoken fizzled in the air as Salvio felt a leap of something he couldn't define. The hardness in his groin was familiar but the sudden clench of his heart was not. Was it lust? His mouth twisted. Of course it was lust—for what else could it be? It just happened to be more powerful than usual because it had taken him by surprise.

Yet there was no answering hunger in her quiet, grey gaze—something which perplexed him, for when *didn't* a woman look at him with desire in her eyes? She was wary, he found himself thinking, with a flicker of amusement. Almost as if she were silently reproaching him for his insolent appraisal—and maybe that sentiment was richly deserved. What *was* he doing survey-ing her curvy body, like a boy from a single-sex school who was meeting a beautiful woman for the first time?

'You're the cook?' he questioned, trying to redeem himself with a safe, if rather banal question.

She nodded. 'Sort of. Officially, I'm the housekeeper but I do a bit of everything. Answer the door to guests and make sure their rooms are serviced, that sort of thing.' She pushed the coffee towards him. 'Will there be anything else, Signor De Gennaro?'

He smiled. 'Salvio. And you are?'

She looked taken aback, as if people didn't ask her name very often. 'It's Molly,' she answered shyly, in a voice so soft it felt like silk lingerie brushing against his skin. 'Molly Miller.'

Molly Miller. He found himself wanting to repeat it, but the conversation—such as it was—was terminated by the sudden sweep of car headlights arcing powerfully across the room. As he heard the sound of a large car swishing over gravel, Salvio saw the way she flinched and automatically tugged at her drab dress so that it hung more uniformly over her wide hips.

'That's the Averys.'

'I thought it must be.'

'You'd better… You'd better go,' she said, unable to keep the waver of urgency from her voice. 'I'm sup-posed to be preparing dinner and Lady Avery won't like finding a guest in the kitchen.'

Salvio was tempted to tell her that he didn't give a damn what Lady Avery would or wouldn't like but he could see the fear which had darkened her soft grey eyes. With a flicker of irritation he picked up his espresso and water and headed for the door. *'Grazie mille,'* he said, leaving the warm and steamy kitchen and walking rapidly towards the staircase, reluctant to be around when the Averys burst into the hallway.

But once back in his own room, he was irritated to discover that the low burn of desire was refusing to leave him. So that instead of the hot shower he'd promised himself, Salvio found himself standing beneath jets of punishingly cold water as he tried to push the curves of the sweet little housekeeper from the forefront of his mind and to quell the exquisite hardness which throbbed at his groin.

CHAPTER TWO

'MOLLY, THESE POTATOES are frightful. We can't possibly ask Signor De Gennaro to eat them. Have they even *seen* an oven? They're like rocks!'

Molly could feel herself flushing to the roots of her hair as she met Lady Avery's accusing stare. Were they? She blinked. Surely she'd blasted them for the required time, carefully basting them with goose fat to make them all golden and crispy? But no. Now she stopped to look at them properly—they were definitely on the anaemic side.

She could feel her cheeks growing even pinker as she reached towards the table to pick up the dish. 'I'm so sorry, Lady Avery. I'll pop them back in the—'

'Don't bother!' snapped her employer. 'It will be midnight before they're fit to eat and I don't intend going to bed on a full stomach. And I'm sure Salvio won't want to either.'

Was it Molly's imagination, or did Lady Avery shoot the Italian a complicit smile from the other side of the table? The way she said his name sounded unmistakably predatory and the look she was giving him was enough to make Molly's stomach turn. Surely the aristocrat wasn't hinting that she intended ending up in bed with him, not with her husband sitting only a few feet away?

Yet it had struck her as odd when Sarah Avery had come down for dinner wearing the tightest and lowest-cut dress imaginable, so that the priceless blaze of the Avery diamonds dazzled like stars against her aging skin. She'd been flirting outrageously with the Italian businessman ever since Molly had served pre-dinner drinks and showed no sign of stopping. And meanwhile, her husband—two decades older and already a quarter of the way through his second bottle of burgundy—seemed oblivious to the undercurrents which had been swirling around the dinner table ever since they'd sat down.

The meal had been a disaster from the moment she'd put the starters on the table and Molly couldn't understand why. She was a good cook. She knew that. Hadn't she spent years cooking for her mother and little brother, trying to produce tasty food on a shoestring budget? And hadn't part of her job interview for Lady Avery consisted of producing a full afternoon tea—including a rich and rather heavy fruit cake—within the space of just two hours…a feat she had managed with ease? A simple meal for just three people should have been a breeze, but Molly hadn't factored in Salvio De Gennaro, or the effect his brooding presence would have on her employer. Or, if she was being honest, on her.

After he'd swept out of the kitchen earlier that afternoon, it had taken ages for her heart to stop thumping

and to be able to concentrate on what she was supposed to be doing. She'd felt all giddy and stupidly...
excited. She remembered the way he had looked into
her eyes with that dark and piercing gaze and wondered
if she'd imagined the pulsing crackle of electricity between them before telling herself that, yes, of course
she had. Unless she really thought a man who could
have his pick of any woman on the planet would have
the slightest interest in a naïve country girl who was
carrying far too much weight around her hips.

In her dreams!

But there was no doubt that Salvio's unexpected trip
to the kitchen had rocked Molly's equilibrium and after
he'd gone, all the light had seemed to disappear from
the room. She'd sat down at the table feeling flat, which
was unusual for her because she'd always tried to be
an optimist, no matter what life threw at her. She was
what was known as a glass-half-full type of person
rather than one who regarded the glass as half empty.
So why had she spent the rest of the afternoon mooch-
ing around the kitchen in a way which was completely
out of character?

'Molly? Are you listening to a word I'm saying?'

Molly stiffened as she saw the fury in Lady Avery's eyes—but not before she'd noticed Salvio De
Gennaro's face darken with an expression she couldn't
work out. Was he wondering why on earth the wife
of a famous peer bothered employing such a hapless
housekeeper?

'I'm so sorry,' said Molly quickly. 'I was a bit distracted.'

'You seem to have been distracted all afternoon!' snapped Lady Avery. 'The meat is overcooked and the hors d'oeuvres were fridge-cold!'

'Come on, Sarah. It's no big deal,' said Salvio softly. 'Give the girl a break.'

Molly's head jerked up and as she met the understanding gleam of Salvio De Gennaro's ebony eyes, she felt something warm and comforting wash over her. It was like sitting beside a fire when snow was falling outside. Like being wrapped in a soft, cashmere blanket. She saw Lady Avery appear momentarily disconcerted and she wondered if Salvio De Gennaro's silky intervention had made her decide that giving her housekeeper a public dressing-down wouldn't reflect very well on *her*. Was that why she flashed her a rather terrifying smile?

'Of course. You're quite right, Salvio. It's no big deal. After all, it's not as if we're short of food, is it? Molly always makes sure we're very well fed, but—as you can tell—she's very fond of her food!' She gave a bright, high laugh and nodded her head towards the snoring form of her husband, who had now worked his way through the entire bottle of wine and whose head was slumped on his chest as he snored softly. 'Molly, I'm going to wake Lord Avery and guide him to bed and then Signor De Gennaro and I will go and sit by the fire in the library. Perhaps you'd like to bring us something on a tray to take the place of dinner. Nothing too fussy. Finger food will do.' She flashed another toothy smile. 'And bring us another bottle of the Château Lafite, will you?'

'Yes, Lady Avery.'

Salvio's knuckles tightened as he watched Molly scuttle from the room, though he made no further comment as his hostess moved round the table to rouse her sleeping husband and then rather impatiently ushered him from the room. But he couldn't shake off the feeling of injustice he had experienced when he'd seen how the aristocrat treated the blushing housekeeper. Or the powerful feeling of identification which had gripped him as he'd witnessed it. Was it because he'd known exactly how she would be feeling? His mouth hardened. Because he'd been where she had been. He knew what it was like to be at the bottom of the food chain. To have people treat you as if you were a machine, rather than a person.

He splayed his fingers over the rigid tautness of his thighs. He would wait until his hostess returned. Force himself to have a quick drink since she'd asked for one of the world's most expensive wines to be opened, then retire to his room. He glanced at his watch. It was too late to go back to London tonight but he would leave at first light, before the house was awake. All in all it had been a wasted journey, with Lord Avery too inebriated to talk business before dinner. He hadn't even been able to work because the damned Internet kept going down and because his thoughts kept straying to the forbidden... And the forbidden had proved shockingly difficult to erase from his mind. He sighed. How crazy was it that the wholesome housekeeper had inexplicably set his senses on fire, so that he could think of little but her?

He'd walked into the orangery before dinner to see her standing with a tray of champagne in her hands. She had changed into a simple black dress which hugged her body and emphasised every voluptuous curve. With her shiny brown hair caught back at the nape of her neck, his attention had been caught by those grey eyes, half concealed by lashes like dark feathers, which were modestly lowered as she offered him a drink. Even that was a turn-on. Or maybe especially that. He wasn't used to modesty. To women reluctant to meet his gaze, whose cheeks turned the colour of summer roses. He'd found himself wanting to stand there studying her and it had taken a monumental effort to tear his eyes away. To try to make conversation with a host who seemed to be having a love affair with the bottle, and his disenchanted wife who was almost spilling out of a dress much too young for a woman her age.

'Salvio!' Sarah Avery was back, a look of determination on her face as she picked her way across the Persian rug on her spiky black heels. 'Sorry about that. I'm afraid that sometimes Philip simply can't hold his drink. Some men can't, you know—with predictable effects, I'm afraid.' She flashed him a megawatt smile. 'Let's go to the library for a drink, shall we?'

There had been many reasons why Salvio had left Naples to make his life in England and he had absorbed the attitudes of his adopted country with the tenacity he applied to every new challenge which came his way. These days he considered himself urbane and sophisticated—but in reality the traditional values of his Neapolitan upbringing were never far from the surface. And in his world, a woman never criticised her husband to another person. Particularly a stranger.

'Just one drink,' he said, disapproval making his words harsher than he intended. 'I have a busy schedule tomorrow and I'll be leaving first thing.'

'But you've only just arrived!'

'And I have back-to-back meetings in London, from midday onwards,' he countered smoothly.

'Oh! Can't you cancel them?' she wheedled. 'I mean, I've heard that you're a complete workaholic, but surely even powerhouses like you are allowed to slow down a little. And this is a beautiful part of the world. You haven't really seen any of it.'

With an effort, Salvio forced a smile because he found her attitude intensely intrusive, as well as irritating. 'I like to honour my commitments,' he observed coolly as he followed her into the firelit library, where Molly was putting cheese and wine on a table, the stiff set of her shoulders showing her tension. He wasn't surprised. Imagine being stuck out here, working for someone as rude and demanding as Sarah Avery. He sank into one of the armchairs, and watched as his hostess went to stand by the mantelpiece in a pose he suspected was intended to make him appreciate her carefully preserved body. She ran one slow finger over the gleaming curve of an ancient-looking vase, and smiled.

'Are you looking forward to Christmas, Salvio?' she questioned.

He was immediately wary—recoiling from the thought that some unwanted invitation might soon be heading his way. 'I am away for most of it—in Naples,' he said, accepting a glass of wine from Molly—ridiculously pleased to capture her blushing gaze before she quickly turned away. 'I'm always glad to see my family but, to be honest, I'm equally glad when the holiday is over. The world shuts down and business suffers as a result.'

'Oh, you men!' Sarah Avery slunk back across the room to perch on a nearby chair, her bony knees clamped tightly together. 'You're all the same!'

Salvio managed not to wince, trying to steer the conversation onto a more neutral footing as he sipped his wine, though all he could think about was Molly hovering nervously in the background, the black dress clinging to her curvaceous figure and a stray strand of glossy brown hair dangling alluringly against her pink cheek. He cleared his throat. 'How are you and your husband planning to spend Christmas?' he questioned politely.

This was obviously the opportunity Sarah Avery had been waiting for and she let him have the answer in full, telling him how much Philip's adult children hated her and blamed her for ending their parents' marriage. 'I mean, I certainly didn't set out to get him, but I was his secretary and these things happen.' She gave a helpless shrug. 'Philip told me he couldn't help falling in love with me. That no power on earth could have stopped it. How was I supposed to know his wife was pregnant at the time?' She sipped a mouthful of wine, leaving a thin red stain above the line of her lip gloss. 'I mean, I really don't care if his wretched kids won't see me— it's Philip I'm concerned about—and I really think they need to be mindful of their inheritance. He'll cut them off if they're not careful!'

Salvio forced himself to endure several minutes more of her malicious chatter, his old-fashioned sensibilities outraged by her total lack of shame. But eventually he could stand no more and rose to his feet and, despite all her cajoling, she finally seemed to get the message that he was going to bed. Alone. Like a child, she pouted, but he paid her sulky expression no heed. He felt like someone who'd just been released from the cage of a prowling she-cat by the time he escaped to the quietness of the guest corridor and closed the door of his room behind him.

A sigh of relief left his lips as he looked around. A fire had been lit and red and golden lights from the flames were dancing across the walls. He'd been in these grand houses before and often found them unbearably cold, but this high-ceilinged room was deliciously warm. Over by the window was a polished antique cabinet on which stood an array of glittering crystal decanters, filled with liquor which glinted in the moonlight. He studied the walls, which were studded with paintings, including some beautiful landscapes by well-known artists. Salvio's mouth twisted. It was ironic really. This house contained pictures which would have been given pride of place in a national gallery—yet a trip to the bathroom required a walk along an icy corridor, because the idea of en-suite was still an alien concept to some members of the aristocracy.

He yawned but didn't go straight to bed, preferring to half pack his small suitcase so he was ready to leave first thing. Outside he could see dark clouds scudding across the sky and partially obscuring the moon, turning the churning ocean silver and black. It was stark and it was beautiful but he was unable to appreciate it because he was restless and didn't know why.

Loosening his tie and undoing the top button of his shirt, Salvio braved the chilly corridor to the bathroom and was on his way back when he heard a sound from the floor above. A sound which at first he didn't recognise. He stilled as he listened and there it was again. His eyes narrowed as he realised what it was. A faint gasp for breath, followed by a snuffle.

Someone was crying?

He told himself it was none of his business. He was leaving first thing and it made sense to go straight to bed. But something tugged at his... He frowned. His conscience? Because he knew that the person crying must be the little housekeeper? He didn't question what made him start walking towards the sound and soon found himself mounting a narrow staircase at the far end of the corridor.

The sound grew louder. Definitely tears. His foot creaked on a step and an anxious voice called out.

'Who's there?'

'It's me. Salvio.'

He heard footsteps scurrying across the room and as the door was pulled open, there stood Molly. She was still wearing her black uniform although she had taken down her hair and removed her sturdy shoes. It spilled over her shoulders in a glorious tumble which fell almost to her waist and Salvio was reminded of a painting he'd once seen of a woman sitting in a boat, with fear written all over her features. He could see fear now, in soft grey eyes which were rimmed with red. And suddenly all the lust he'd felt from the moment he'd set eyes on her was replaced by a powerful sense of compassion.

'What's happened?' he demanded. 'Are you hurt?'

'Nothing's happened and, no, I'm not hurt.' Quickly, she blotted her cheeks with her fingertips. 'Did you want something?' she asked, a familiar note of duty creeping into her voice. 'I hope... I mean, is everything in your room to your satisfaction, Signor De Gennaro?'

'Everything in my room is fine and I thought I told you to call me Salvio,' he said impatiently. 'I want to know why you were crying.'

She shook her head. 'I wasn't crying.'

'Yes, you were. You know damned well you were.'

An unexpected streak of defiance made her tilt her chin upwards. 'Surely I'm allowed to cry in the privacy of my own room.'

'And surely I'm allowed to ask why, if it's keeping me awake.'

Her grey eyes widened. 'Was it?'

He allowed himself the flicker of a smile. 'Well, no—now you come to mention it. Not really. I hadn't actually gone to bed but it's not a sound anyone particularly wants to hear.'

'That's because nobody was supposed to. Look, I'm really sorry to have disturbed you, but I'm fine now. See.' This time she gritted her teeth into a parody of a smile. 'It won't happen again.'

But Salvio's interest was piqued and the fact that she was trying to get rid of him intrigued him. He glanced over her shoulder at her room, which was small. He hadn't seen a bedroom that small for a long time. A narrow, unfriendly bed and thin drapes at the window, but very little else. Suddenly he became aware of the icy temperature—an observation which was reinforced by the almost imperceptible shiver she gave, despite the thickness of her black dress. He thought about the fire in his own bedroom with the blazing applewood logs which she must have lit herself.

'You're cold,' he observed.

'Only a bit. I'm used to it. You know what these old houses are like. The heating is terrible up here.'

'You don't say?' He narrowed his eyes speculatively. 'Look, why don't you come and sit by my fire for a while? Have a nightcap, perhaps.'

She narrowed her eyes. 'A nightcap?'

He slanted her a mocking smile. 'You know. The drink traditionally supposed to warm people up.'

He saw her hesitate before shaking her head.

'Look, it's very kind of you to offer, but I can't possibly accept.'

'Why not?'

'Because...' She shrugged. 'You know why not.'

'Not unless you tell me, I don't.'

'Because Lady Avery would hit the roof if she caught me socialising with one of the guests.'

'And how's she going to find out?' he questioned with soft complicity. 'I won't tell if you won't. Come on, Molly. You're shivering. What harm will it do?'

Molly hesitated because she *was* tempted—more tempted than she should have been. Maybe it was because she was feeling so cold—both inside and out. A coldness she'd been unable to shift after the telling off she'd just been given by Lady Avery, who had arrived in the kitchen in an evil temper, shaking with rage as she'd shouted at Molly. She'd told her she was clumsy and incompetent. That she'd never been so ashamed in her life and no wonder Signor De Gennaro had cut short the evening so unexpectedly.

Yet now that same man was standing in the doorway of her humble room, asking her to have a drink with him. He had removed his tie and undone the top button of his shirt, giving him a curiously relaxed and accessible air. It was easy to see why Lady Avery had made a fool of herself over him during dinner. Who wouldn't fall for his olive-dark skin and gleaming ebony eyes?

Yet despite his sexy appearance, he had looked at her understandingly when she'd messed up during dinner. He'd come to her rescue—and there was that same sense of concern on his face now. He had an unexpected streak of kindness, she thought, and kindness was hard to resist. Especially when you weren't expecting it. An icy blast of wind rushed in through the gap in the window frame and once again Molly shivered. The days ahead didn't exactly fill her with joy and her worries about Robbie were never far from the surface. Couldn't she loosen up for once in her life? Break out of the lonely mould she'd created for herself by having a drink with the Italian tycoon?

She gave a tentative shrug. 'Okay, then. I will. Just

a quick one, mind. And thank you,' she added, as she slipped her feet back into the sensible brogues she'd just kicked off. 'Thank you very much.'

He gave a brief nod, as if her agreement was something he'd expected all along, and Molly tried to tell herself that this meant nothing special—at least, not to him. But as he turned his back and began to walk she realised her heart was racing and Molly was filled with an unfamiliar kind of excitement as she followed Salvio De Gennaro along the narrow corridor towards his grand bedroom on the floor below.

CHAPTER THREE

'HERE.'

'Thanks.' Molly took the brandy Salvio was offering her, wondering if she'd been crazy to accept his invitation to have a drink with him, because now she was in his room she felt hopelessly embarrassed and out of place. She noticed his half-packed open suitcase lying on the far side of the room and, for some stupid reason, her heart sank. He obviously couldn't wait to get away from here. Awkwardly, she shifted from one foot to the other.

'Why don't you sit down over there, beside the fire?' he suggested.

Lowering herself into the chair he'd indicated, Molly thought how weird it was to find herself in the role of visitor to a room she had cleaned so many times. Just this morning she'd been in here, fluffing up the new duvet and making sure the monogrammed pillowcases were all neatly facing in the right direction. Over there were the neat stack of freshly ironed newspapers Lady Avery had insisted on, and the jug of water with the little lace cover on top. Yet it was funny how quickly you could get used to the dramatic change from servant to guest. The soft leather of the armchair felt deliciously soft as it sank beneath her weight and the warmth of the fire licked her skin. She took a tentative sip from her glass, recoiling a little as the powerful fumes wafted upwards.

'Not much of a drinker?' observed Salvio wryly, as he poured his own drink.

'Not really.' But even that minuscule amount of liquor had started to dissolve the tight knot of tension in the pit of her stomach, sending a warm glow flooding through her body. Molly stared out of the windows where clouds were racing across the silvery face of the moon. Outside the temperature had plummeted but in here it felt cosy—in fact, she might even go so far as to say she was starting to feel relaxed. Yet here she was in a strange man's bedroom in her black uniform and heavy-duty shoes as if she had every right to be there. What on earth would Lady Avery say if she happened to walk in? Anxiety rippled through her as she glanced at Salvio, who was replacing the heavy stopper in the bottle. 'I really shouldn't be here,' she fretted.

'So you said,' he drawled, his tinge of boredom implying that he found repetition tedious. 'But you are here. And you still haven't told me why you were crying.'

'I...' She took another sip of brandy before putting the glass down on a nearby table. 'No reason really.'

'Now, why don't I believe you, Molly Miller?' he challenged softly. 'What happened? Did you get into more trouble about dinner?'

Her startled expression told Salvio his guess was correct. 'I deserved it,' she said flatly as she met his gaze. 'The meal was rubbish.'

Briefly he acknowledged her loyalty. She would have been perfectly justified in moaning about her employer but she hadn't. She was a curious creature, he thought, his gaze flickering over her dispassionately. Totally without artifice, she didn't seem to care that the way she was sitting wasn't the most flattering angle she could have chosen. Yet her abundant hair glowed like copper in the firelight and as she crossed one ankle over the other he was surprised by how unexpectedly erotic that simple movement seemed. But he hadn't brought her here to seduce her, he reminded himself sternly. Tonight he had cast himself in the role of the good Samaritan, that was all. 'And that's the only reason for your tears?'

Molly gave an awkward wriggle of her shoulders. 'Maybe I was feeling sorry for myself,' she admitted, shifting beneath his probing gaze. Because no way was she going to tell him the real reason. He wouldn't be interested in her wayward brother or his habit of accumulating debt, but more than that—she was afraid of saying the words out loud. As if saying them would make them even more real. She didn't want to wonder why Robbie had rung up just an hour ago, asking her if she had any spare cash for a 'temporary' loan, despite his promises to find himself some sort of job. Why hadn't he got any money of his own? Why was he asking her for more, after all his tearful promises that from now on he was going to live his life independently and free of debt? She swallowed. She couldn't bear to think that he'd got himself into that terrible spiral yet again—of playing poker and losing. Of owing money to hard-faced men who wouldn't think twice about scarring his pretty young face...

'Call it a touch of self-pity,' she said, meeting the black fire in his eyes and realising he was still waiting for an answer. 'Not something I imagine you have much experience of.'

Salvio gave a mirthless smile. How touching her faith in him! Did she think that because he was wealthy and successful, he had never known pain or despair, when he had been on intimate terms with both those things? His mouth hardened. When his life had imploded and he'd lost everything, he remembered the darkness which had descended on him, sending him hurtling into a deep and never-ending hole. And even though he'd dragged himself out of the quagmire and forced himself to start over—you never forgot an experience like that. It marked you. Changed you. Turned you into someone different. A stranger to yourself as well as to those around you. It was why he had left Naples—because he couldn't bear to be reminded of his own failure. 'Why do you stay here?' he questioned quietly.

'It's a very well-paid job.'

'Even though you get spoken to like that?'

She shook her head, her long hair swaying like a glossy curtain. 'It's not usually as bad as it was tonight.'

'Your loyalty is touching, *signorina*.'

'I'm paid to be loyal,' she said doggedly.

'I'm sure you are. But even taking all that into account, this place is very *isolato*...isolated.' He gave a flicker of a smile, as if begging her to forgive his sudden lapse into his native tongue. 'I can't imagine many people your age living nearby.'

'Maybe that's one of the reasons I like it.'

He raised his eyebrows. 'You don't like to socialise?'

Molly hesitated. Should she tell him that she always felt out of place around people her own age? That she didn't really do the relaxed stuff, or the fun stuff, or the wild stuff. She'd spent too many years caring for her mother and then trying to keep her brother from going off the rails—and that kind of sensible role could become so much a part of you that it was difficult to relinquish it. And wouldn't that kind of admission bring reality crashing into the room? Wouldn't it puncture the slightly unreal atmosphere which had descended on her ever since she'd walked in here and settled down by the fireside, allowing herself to forget for a short while that she was Molly the housekeeper—so that for once she'd felt like a person in her own right?

'I can take people or leave them,' she said. 'Anyway, socialising is expensive and I'm saving up. I'm intending to put my brother through college and it isn't cheap. He's in Australia at the moment,' she explained, in answer to the fractional rise of his dark brows. 'Doing a kind of...gap year.'

He frowned. 'So you're here—working hard—while he has fun in the sun? That's a very admirable sacrifice for a sister to make.'

'Anyone would do it.'

'Not anyone, no. He's lucky to have you.'

Molly picked up her glass again and took another sip of brandy. Would Salvio De Gennaro be shocked if he knew the truth? That Robbie hadn't actually got a place at college yet, because he was still 'thinking about it', in spite of all her entreaties to get himself a proper education and not end up like her. She licked her lips, which tasted of brandy. She didn't want to think about Robbie. Surely she could have a night off for once? A night when she could feel young and carefree and revel in the fact that she was alone with a gorgeous man like Salvio—even if he had only invited her here because he felt sorry for her.

Putting her glass down, she stared at him and her heart gave a sudden lurch of yearning. He hadn't moved from his spot by the window and his powerful body was starkly outlined by the moonlight.

'What about you?' she questioned suddenly. 'What brought you here?'

He shrugged. 'I was supposed to be discussing a deal with Philip Avery.' He twisted his lips into a wry smile. 'But that doesn't look like it's going to happen.'

'He'll be much more receptive in the morning,' said Molly diplomatically.

'It'll be too late by then,' he said. 'I'm leaving as soon as it's light.'

Molly was aware of a crushing sense of disappointment. She'd wanted... She stared very hard at her brandy glass as if the dark amber liquid would provide the answer. What had she wanted? To see him at breakfast—their eyes meeting in a moment of shared complicity as they remembered this illicit, night-time drink?

'Oh, that's a shame,' she said, sounding genuinely disappointed.

He smiled, as if her earnestness had amused him. 'You know, you're far too sweet to be hiding yourself away somewhere like this, Molly.'

Sweet. Molly knew it was a compliment yet for some reason it offended her. It made her sound like the cake he'd caught her eating. Because sweet wasn't sexy, was it? Just as *she* wasn't sexy. 'Am I?' she questioned tone-lessly.

He nodded, walking over to the desk and writing something on the back of a business card before crossing the room and handing it to her. 'Here. Take this. It will get you straight through to my assistant. If ever you decide you want a change, then give her a ring. She knows plenty of people, and domestic staff are always in short supply.' He met her eyes. 'You could always find something better than this, you know.'

'Despite dinner being such a disaster?' She tried to sound jokey even if she didn't feel it, because she re-alised she was being dismissed. Getting up from the comfort of her fireside seat, Molly took the card and slid it into the hip pocket of her dress.

'Despite that,' he agreed, his words suddenly trailing away as his gaze followed the movement of her hand.

Molly became aware of a subtle alteration in the at-mosphere as Salvio lifted his eyes to her face. She'd wondered if the attraction which had sizzled between them earlier had been wishful thinking, but maybe it hadn't. Maybe it had been real. As real as the sudden thrust of her nipples against the soft fabric of her dress and the distracting heat between her thighs. She held her breath, waiting, instinct telling her that he was going to touch her. Despite him being who he was and her being just Molly. And he did. Lifting his hand, he ran the tips of his fingers experimentally over her hair.

'E capelli tuoi so comme a seta,' he said, and when she looked at him in confusion, he translated. 'Your hair is like silk.'

It was the most beautiful thing anyone had ever said to her and when she heard it in Italian it made her want to melt. Was that why he did it, knowing it would push her a little further beneath his powerful spell? Molly told herself to move away. She should thank him for the drink, for his kindness and for giving her his card and then hurry back to her little room to mull over her memories and hug them to her like a hot-water bottle. But she didn't move. She just carried on gazing up into the rugged perfection of his looks, praying he would kiss her and make the fairy tale complete—even if that was all she was ever going to have to remember him by. 'Is—is it?' she questioned.

Salvio smiled, letting his thumb drift from the fire-warmed strands, to hover over the unmistakable tremble of her lips. He felt a tightness in his throat as he realised what he was about to do. He had invited her here because he sensed she was lonely and unhappy—not because he intended to seduce her. Because there were rules and usually he followed them. He no longer took physical comfort just because it was available—because it was pretty much always available to a man like him. Just as he no longer used sex to blot out his pain, or his anger.

But the little housekeeper had touched a part of him

he'd thought had died a long time ago. She had stirred a compassion in his soul and now she was stirring his body in a way which was all too obvious, if only to him. He could feel the aching hardness at his groin, but the urge to kiss her was even more overwhelming than the need to bury himself deep inside her body. He told himself he should resist—gently shoo her out of the door and send her on her way. And maybe he would have done—had she not chosen that moment to expel a shaky breath of air, the warmth of it shuddering softly against his thumb.

How could something as insignificant as a breath be so potent? he marvelled as he stared down into her wide grey eyes. 'I want to kiss you,' he said softly. 'But if that happens I will want to make love to you and I'm not sure that's such a good idea. Do you understand what I'm saying, Molly?'

Wordlessly, she nodded.

'And the only thing which will stop me, is you,' he continued, his voice a deep silken purr. 'So stop me, Molly. Turn away and walk out right now and do us both a favour, because something tells me this is a bad idea.'

He was giving her the opportunity to leave but Molly knew she wasn't going to take it—because when did things like this ever happen to people like her? She wasn't like most women her age. She'd never had sex. Never come even close, despite her few forays onto a dating website, which had all ended in disaster. Yet now a man she barely knew was proposing seduction and suddenly she was up for it, and she didn't care if it was *bad*. Hadn't she spent her whole life trying to be good? And where had it got her?

Her heart was crashing against her ribcage as she stared up into his rugged features and greedily drank them in. 'I don't care if it's a bad idea,' she whispered. 'Maybe I want it as much as you do.'

Her response made him tense. She saw his eyes narrow and heard him utter something which sounded more like despair than joy before pulling her almost roughly into his arms. He smoothed the hair away from her cheeks and lowered his head and the moment their lips met, she knew there would be no turning back.

At first his kiss was slow. As if he was exploring her mouth by touch alone. And just when she was starting to get used to the sheer dreaminess of it, it became hard. Urgent. It fuelled the hunger which was building inside her. He levered her up against him, so that her breasts were thrusting eagerly against his torso and she could feel the rock-hard cradle of his pelvis. She should have been daunted by the unmistakable bulk of his erection but she wasn't, because her hungry senses were controlling her now and she didn't feel like good, rule-following Molly any more. She felt like wanton Molly—a victim of her own desire.

And it felt good.

More than good.

His laugh was unsteady as he splayed his fingers over one of her breasts, the nipple instantly hardening against his palm. 'You are very passionate,' he murmured.

Molly gave a small gurgle of pleasure as he found the side zip of her dress because suddenly she *felt* passionate. As if she had been waiting all her life to feel this way. 'Am I?'

'I don't think you need any reassurance on that score, *bedda mia.*'

He was wrong, of course—but he wasn't to know that and Molly certainly wasn't going to tell him. She felt breathless as he peeled the plain black dress away from her body and let it fall to the ground before stepping back to survey her. And wasn't it funny how a look of admiration in a man's eyes could be powerful enough to dispel all a woman's instinctive insecurities? Because for once Molly wasn't thinking that her tummy was too plump or her breasts unfashionably massive. Or even that her bra didn't match her rather functional pants. Instead she was revelling in the look of naked hunger which made his eyes resemble black fire as they blazed over her.

And then he picked her up. Picked her up! She could hardly believe it. He was carrying chunky Molly Miller towards the bed as if she weighed no more than a balloon at a child's birthday party, before whipping back the brand-new duvet she'd purchased that very morning and depositing her beneath it. It was the most delicious sensation in the world, sinking into the mattress and lying beneath the warmth of the bedding, her body sizzling with a growing excitement—while Salvio De Gennaro began to undress. She swallowed, completely hypnotised as she watched him. The shoes and socks were first to go and then he unbuttoned his shirt, baring his magnificent chest before turning his attention to the zip of his trousers. But when he hooked his thumb inside the waistband of his boxers, Molly squeezed her eyes tightly closed.

'No. Not like that. Open your eyes. Look at me,' he instructed softly and she was too much in thrall to disobey him.

Molly swallowed. She couldn't deny that it was slightly daunting to see just how aroused he was and as she bit her lip, he smiled.

'*Me fai asci pazzo,*' he said, as if that explained everything.

'Wh-what does that mean?'

'It means you make me crazy.'

'I love it when you talk Italian to me,' she said shyly.

'Not Italian,' he said sternly as he slipped into bed beside her. 'Neapolitan.'

She blinked. 'It's different?'

'It's dialect,' he said and she noticed he was placing several foil packets on the antique chest of drawers beside the bed. 'And yes, it's very different.'

The appearance of condoms somehow punctured some of the romance, but by then he was naked beside her and Molly was discovering that the sensation of skin touching skin was like nothing she'd ever known. It was *heaven.* Better than chocolate cake. Better than... well, anything really.

'Salvio,' she breathed, trying out his name for the first time.

'*Sì, bedda mia?* Want me to kiss you again?'

'Yes, please,' she said fervently, and he laughed.

His kisses were deep. It felt as if he were drugging her with them, making her body receptive to the caress of his fingers. And, oh, those fingers—what magic they worked as he tiptoed them over her shivering flesh. He massaged her peaking nipples until she was writhing with pleasure, and when he slid his hand between her thighs and discovered how wet she was, he had to silence her instinctive gasp with another kiss.

And because she didn't want to be passive, Molly stroked him back. At first she was cautious—concentrating on his chest and ribcage, before daring to explore a belly which was far flatter than her own. But when she plucked up the courage to touch the unfamiliar hardness which kept brushing against her quivering thigh, he stopped her with a stern look. 'No.'

She didn't ask him why. She didn't dare. She was afraid of doing anything which would shatter the mood or show how inexperienced she really was. Which might make Salvio De Gennaro bolt upright in bed and incredulously question what the hell he was doing, being intimate with a humble housekeeper. But he didn't. In fact, he seemed just as in tune with her body as she was with his. Like greedy animals, they rolled uninhibitedly around on the bed, biting and nipping and stroking and moaning and there was only the briefest hiatus when Salvio reached for one of the foil packets.

'Want to put this on for me?' he questioned provocatively. 'Since my hands are shaking so much I'm beginning to wonder if I can manage to do it myself.'

Some of Molly's composure left her. Should she say something?

Salvio, I've only ever seen a condom in a biology class at school. I've never actually used one for real.

Mightn't learning that send him hurtling out of bed in horror? Yes, he might be as aroused as she imagined any man *could* be, but even so…mightn't it be a bit heavy if she burdened him with a piece of knowledge which wasn't really relevant? After all, it wasn't as if she was expecting this…interlude to actually go anywhere.

And maybe he read her thoughts because he brought his face up close to hers and surveyed her with smoky eyes. 'You know that I—'

'Yes, I know. You're leaving in the morning,' she said. 'And that's okay.'

'You're sure?'

'Quite sure. I just want…'

'What do you want, Molly?' he questioned, almost gently.

'I just want tonight,' she breathed. 'That's all.'

Salvio frowned as he stroked on a condom. Was she for real, or just too good to be true? He kissed her again, wanting to explode with hunger but forcing himself to move as slowly as possible as he pushed inside her molten heat, because he was big. He'd been told that often enough in the past but he had never felt bigger than he did tonight.

But size had nothing to do with her next reaction. The tensing of her body and her brief grimace of pain told their own unbelievable story. Confusion swirled his thoughts and made him momentarily still. With an almighty effort he prepared to withdraw, but somehow her tight muscles clamped themselves around him in a way which was shockingly new and exciting, making him dangerously close to coming straight away.

He sucked in a raw breath, trying desperately to claw back control. Trying to concentrate on not giving in to his orgasm, rather than on the unbelievable fact that the housekeeper was a virgin. Or rather, she *had* been.

But stopping himself from coming was the hardest sexual test he'd ever set himself. Maybe it was her tightness which felt so delicious. Or the uninhibited way she was responding to him. She was a stranger to all the games usually played in the bedroom, he realised—and her naivety made her an unmatchable lover, because she was a natural. She hadn't learnt any tricks or manoeuvres. The things she was doing she hadn't done with any other man before and somehow that turned him on. He revelled in the way she squirmed those fleshy hips as he drove into her. The way she thrust her breast towards his lips, so that he could tease the pointing nipple with first his tongue and then his teeth. He sensed the change in her—the moment when her orgasm became inevitable—and he watched her closely, seeing her dark eyelashes flutter to a close. Triumph washed over him as she made that first disbelieving choke of pleasure and a rosy flush began to blossom over her breasts. And only when the last of her violent spasms had died away did he give in to his own need, unprepared for the power of what was happening to him. It felt like the first time, he thought dazedly. Or maybe the only time.

And then he fell asleep.

CHAPTER FOUR

IT WAS STILL dark when Salvio awoke next morning—the illuminated dial of his wristwatch informing him it was just past six. He waited a moment until his eyes became adjusted to the shadows in the bedroom. In the heat of that frantic sexual encounter which had taken him almost by surprise last night, he hadn't bothered to close the drapes and outside it was still dark—but then, sunrise came late to this part of the world in the depths of an English winter.

He glanced across at the sleeping woman beside him, sucking in a slow lungful of air as he tried to get his head around what had happened. Trying to justify the fact that he'd had sex with the innocent housekeeper, when deep down he knew there could be no justification. Yet she had wanted it, he reminded himself grimly. She had wanted it as much as him.

They had been intimate again during the night—several times, as it happened. His stretching leg had encountered the voluptuous softness of her warm flesh, making him instantly aroused. There had been a stack of questions he'd been meaning to ask, but somehow her touch had wiped them from his mind. The second time had been amazing—and so had the third. She was so easy to please. So grateful for the pleasure he gave her. He'd expected her to start bringing up tricky topics after orgasm number five, but his expectations hadn't materialised. She hadn't demanded to know if he had changed his mind about seeing her again, which was fortunate really, because he hadn't. His eyes narrowed. He couldn't. She was too sweet. Too naïve. She wouldn't last a minute in his world and his own cynical nature would destroy all that naïve enthusiasm of hers in an instant.

Leaning over, he shook her bare shoulder—resisting the desire to slip his hand beneath the duvet and begin massaging one of those magnificent breasts.

'Molly,' he murmured. 'Wake up. It's morning.'

It was a shock for Molly to open her eyes and realise she was staring up at the magnificent chandelier which hung from the ceiling of the guest bedroom. In this faint light it twinkled like the fading stars outside the window and she forced herself to remember that in several hours' time she would be attacking it with her feather duster, not lying beneath the priceless shards of crystal, with the warm body of a naked man beside her.

A shiver ran through her as she turned her head to look at Salvio, her heart punching out a violent beat as she realised what she'd done. She swallowed. What *hadn't* she done? She had let him undress her and explore every inch of her body, with his tongue and his fingers and a whole lot more beside. When he'd been deep inside her body, she had choked out his name over and over again as he had awoken an appetite she hadn't realised she possessed. Somehow he had waved a magic wand and turned her into someone she didn't really recognise and she had gone from being inexperienced Molly Miller, to an eager woman who couldn't get enough of him. Briefly she closed her eyes.

And she wasn't going to regret a single second of it. Because you couldn't turn the clock back—and even if you could, who would want to?

She yawned, stretching her arms above her head and registering the unfamiliar aching of her body. How many times had he made love to her? she wondered dazedly, as she recalled his seemingly insatiable appetite and her own eager response.

She forced herself to ask the question she didn't really want to ask. 'What time is it?'

'Just after six.' There was a pause. His eyes became hooded. 'Molly—'

'Well, you'd better get going, hadn't you?' Her breezy interjection forestalled him because she'd guessed what he was about to say—the heaviness of his tone warning her that this was the Big Goodbye. And he didn't need to. He had to go and she was okay with that. Why ruin everything by demanding more than he'd ever intended to give? She pinned an efficient smile to her lips. 'You did say you wanted to get away early.'

He frowned, as if her response wasn't what he'd been expecting, but Molly knew there was only one way to deal with a situation like this, and that was by being sensible, the way she'd been all her life. She had to face facts, not mould them to suit her fantasies. She knew there could be no future between her and the billionaire tycoon because their lives were too different. Last night the boundaries had become blurred—but one night of bliss didn't change the fundamentals, did it? She was employed as a housekeeper—and lying in an honoured guest's bed was the very last place she should be.

'You're sure you're okay?' he growled.

She wondered where the rogue thought came from. The one which made her want to say, *Not really, no. I wish you could take me with you wherever you're going and make love to me the way you did last night.*

But fortunately, the practical side of her character was the dominant one. As if Salvio De Gennaro would want to take her away with him! She tried to imagine cramming herself into that low-slung sports car— why, her weight would probably disable the suspension! 'Why wouldn't I be okay?' she questioned breezily. 'It was great. At least, I think it was.' For the first time, a trace of insecurity crept into her voice as she looked at him with a question in her eyes.

'Oh, it was more than "great",' he affirmed, reaching out to trace the tip of his finger over the quiver of her bottom lip. 'In fact, it was so good that I want to do it all over again.'

Once again Molly felt her stomach clench with desire and a rush of heat tugged deep inside her. 'But...' she whispered as he moved closer.

'But what, *mia bedda*?'

'There isn't...' She swallowed. 'There isn't time.'

'Says who?'

He slipped his hand between her legs. Molly wondered what had happened to the sensible part of her now. Forgotten, that was what. Banished by the first lazy stroke of his finger over her slick heat. 'Salvio,' she moaned, as his dark head moved down and his tongue found her nipple.

He lifted his head from her breast, dark eyes gleaming in the half-light. 'You want me to stop?'

'You know I don't,' she gasped.

'So why don't you show me what you *would* like?'

Maybe it was the knowledge that this was the last time which made her so adventurous, because Molly suddenly found her hand drifting over his taut belly to capture the rocky erection which was pressing so insistently against her thigh. 'This,' she said shakily. 'This is what I want.'

'And where do you want it?'

'In me,' she breathed boldly. 'Inside me.'

'Me, too,' he purred, reaching out to grab a condom from the sadly diminished pile on the bedside cabinet.

Molly was aware of being warm and sticky as he moved over her. Of her hair all mussed and her teeth unbrushed—but somehow none of that seemed to matter because Salvio was touching her as if she were some kind of goddess. His fingers were sure and seeking and goosebumps rippled over her skin in response as he smoothed his hand over her belly. She felt as if she were *soaring* as she wrapped her thighs around his hips and gave herself up to the exquisite sensation of that first sweet thrust and then the deepening movements which followed.

She loved the way they moved in time. The way she

felt as if she were on a fast shuttle to paradise when another orgasm took her over the top. And she loved his
almost helpless expression as his face darkened and he
pumped his seed inside her. The way his tousled head
collapsed onto her shoulder afterwards as he uttered
something intently in what she presumed was more
Neapolitan dialect. His breathing was warm and even
against her neck and, terrified he would fall asleep and
delay his departure, she shook him. 'Salvio,' she whispered. 'Don't go to sleep. You'd better go. Before anyone wakes up.'

'Then you'd better get out of here, too,' he instructed,
pushing aside the rumpled duvet. 'Right now. Before
anyone sees you.'

For some reason his remark dispirited her and
brought her crashing back to earth, allowing reality to
puncture her little bubble of happiness. But despite the
insecurities which were bubbling up inside her, Molly
managed to retain her cheery smile, enjoying the sight
of Salvio pulling on his jeans and sweater and quietly
opening the door as he headed for the bathroom.

Once he'd gone she got out of bed and pulled on her
discarded underclothes—pulling a face as she smoothed
her crumpled work dress over her hips and rolled her
black tights into a little ball, which she gripped in her
hand. She'd be able to do something with her appearance once Salvio had left, she reasoned—glancing up
as the door opened as he came back into the bedroom,
his dark hair glittering with tiny drops of water from
the shower.

In silence he dressed before snapping his overnight

case closed, his expression very serious as he walked towards her. For a moment he just stood in front of her, his gaze sweeping over her like a dark spotlight, as if he were seeing her for the first time.

'So why?' he questioned simply. 'Why me?

Molly expelled a shuddered breath, because in a way she'd been waiting for this question. He hadn't asked her last night and she'd been glad, because she hadn't wanted the mundane to spoil what had been the most fantastic night of her life. In a way, she would have preferred it if he hadn't brought it up now—but he had, and she needed to answer in a way designed to keep it light. Because she didn't want a single thing to tarnish the memory of how glorious it had been. She shrugged. She even managed a smile. 'I don't meet many men in this line of work,' she said. 'And certainly none like you. And you're...you're a very attractive man, Salvio—as I expect you've been told on many occasions.'

He frowned, as if her honesty troubled him. 'I want you to know that I didn't invite you in here in order to seduce you,' he said slowly. 'I'm not saying the thought hadn't crossed my mind earlier, but that wasn't my intention.'

She nodded. 'I know it wasn't. You were being kind, that's all. Maybe that's why I agreed to have a drink with you.'

He gave an odd kind of laugh. 'You had a very profound effect on me, Molly.'

There was an expression in his dark eyes which Molly couldn't work out but maybe it was best that way. She didn't want him telling her it had been an inexplicable thing he'd done. She wanted to hang onto what had happened between them—to treat it as you would one of those precious baubles you hung on the tree at Christmas. She didn't want to let the memory slip from her fingers and see it shatter into a million pieces.

'I'm glad,' she said, holding onto her composure only by a thread, her heart pounding frantically beneath her breast. 'But time's getting on. You'd better go.'

He nodded, as if being encouraged to leave a bedroom was a novel experience for him, but suddenly he turned and walked towards the bedroom door without another word, and Molly's heart twisted painfully as he closed it quietly behind him. She stood there framed in the window, watching as he emerged from the house, his dark figure silhouetted against the crashing ocean, and for a second he looked up, his black gaze capturing hers. She waited for him to smile, or wave, or something—and she told herself it was best he didn't, for who knew who else might be watching?

Throwing his bag inside, he slipped into the driver's seat, the closing door blotting out her last sight of him. His powerful car started up in a small cloud of gravel before sweeping down towards the coastal road and she watched until it was just a faint black dot in the distance. As sunrise touched the dark clouds with the first hint of red, Molly wondered if Salvio's life was a series of exits, with women gazing longingly out of windows as they watched him go.

Her cheeks were hot as she whipped the bottom sheet from the bed and removed the duvet cover. She would come back later to collect the linen and clean the room from top to bottom. But first she needed a hot shower. The Averys had plenty of events coming up and Molly had a long list of things to do today. Perhaps it was good that the weeks ahead were busy during the run-up to Christmas. It would certainly stop her from dwelling on the fact she would never see Salvio again. Never feel his lips on hers or his powerful arms holding her tight. Because this was what happened in the grown-up world, she told herself fiercely. People had fun with each other. Fun without expectations, or commitment. They had sex and then they just walked away.

Quietly, she closed the guest-room door behind her and was creeping along the corridor with the exaggerated care of a cartoon thief, when she became aware of someone watching her. Her heart lurched with fear. A shadowed figure was standing perfectly still at the far end of the guest corridor.

Not just anyone.

Lady Avery.

Molly's footsteps slowed, her heart crashing frantically against her ribcage as she met the accusing look in her boss's pale eyes.

'So, Molly,' Lady Avery said, in a voice she'd never heard her use before. 'Did you sleep well?'

There was a terrible pause and Molly's throat constricted, because what could she say? It would be adding insult to injury if she made some lame excuse about why she was creeping out of Salvio's room at this time in the morning, carrying a balled-up pair of tights. And now she would be sacked. She'd be jobless and home-

SHARON KENDRICK 59

less at the worst possible time of year. She swallowed.
There was only one thing she *could* say. 'I'm sorry,
Lady Avery.'

Her aristocratic employer shook her head in disbelief. 'I can't believe it!' she said. 'Why someone like
him could have been interested in someone like you,
when he could have had...'

Her words trailed away and Molly didn't dare fill the
awkward silence which followed. Because how could
Lady Avery possibly finish her own sentence without
losing face or dignity? How could she possibly admit
that *she* had been hoping to end up in Salvio's bed,
when she was a married woman and her husband was
in the house?

Molly's cheeks grew hot as she acknowledged the
shameful progression of her thoughts. Behaving as if
the Neapolitan tycoon were some kind of prize they'd
both been competing over! Had the loneliness of her
job made her completely indiscriminate, so that she
had been prepared to leap into bed with the first man
who had ever shown her any real affection? 'I can only
apologise,' she repeated woodenly.

Once again, Lady Avery shook her head. 'Just get
back to work, will you?' she ordered sharply.

'Work?' echoed Molly cautiously.

'Well, what else did you think you'd be doing? We
have ten people coming for dinner tonight, in case you'd
forgotten. And since this time I'm assuming you won't
be obsessing about one of the guests, at least the meat
won't arrive at the table cremated.' She gave Molly
an arch look. 'Unless no man is now safe from your

clutches. I must say you're the most unlikely candidate to be a *femme fatale*. Just get back to work, will you, Molly, before I change my mind?'

'Y-yes, Lady Avery.'

Unable to believe she hadn't been fired on the spot, Molly spent the next few weeks working harder than she'd ever worked before. She went above and beyond the call of duty as Christmas approached and she tried to make amends for her unprofessional behaviour. She attempted ambitious culinary experiments, which thankfully all turned out brilliantly. She baked, prodded, steamed and whipped—to the fervent admiration of the stream of guests which passed through the mistletoe-festooned hallway of the house. And if Lady Avery made a few sarcastic digs about Molly hanging around hopefully beneath the sprigs of white berries, Molly was mature enough not to respond. Maybe her boss's anger was justified, she reasoned. Maybe she would have said the same if the situation had been reversed.

And it didn't matter how busy she was—it was never enough to stop her thoughts from spinning in an unwanted direction. She found herself thinking about Salvio and that was the last thing she needed. She didn't want to remember all the things he'd done to her. The way he'd stroked her face and lips and body, before pushing open her thighs to enter her. Just as she didn't want to think about the way he'd whispered *'bedda mia'* and *'nicuzza'* in that haunting dialect when they'd both woken in the middle of the night. Because remembering that stuff was dangerous. It made it all too easy to imagine that it mattered. And it didn't. Not to him. He'd been able to walk away without a second glance and Molly had told him she was able to do the same.

So do it.

Stop yearning.

Stop wishing for the impossible.

It was four days before Christmas when two bomb-shells fell in rapid succession. Molly had just been about to drive to the village, when she came across Lady Avery standing in the hallway—a full-length fur coat swamping her fine-boned frame. Her face looked cold. As cold as the wintry wind which was whistling outside the big house and bringing with it the first few flakes of snow.

'Molly, don't bother going to the shops right now,' she said, without preamble.

Molly blinked. She'd made the pudding and cake and mince pies, but she still had to pick up the turkey and the vegetables. And hadn't they run out of satsumas? She looked at her boss helpfully. 'Is there something else you would rather I was doing?'

'Indeed there is. You can go upstairs and pack your things.'

Molly stared at her boss in confusion. 'Pack my things?' she echoed stupidly. 'I don't understand.'

'Don't you? It's really quite simple. Surely there's no need for me to spell it out for you. We no longer re-quire your services.'

'But...'

'But what, Molly?' Lady Avery took a step closer and

now Molly could see that all the rage she'd been bottling up since Salvio's departure was about to come spilling out. 'I hope you aren't going to ask me why I haven't given you more notice, because I really don't think the normal rules apply when you've abused your position as outrageously as you have done. I really don't think that *sleeping with the guests* ever made it into your job description, do you?'

'But it's just before Christmas!' Molly burst out, unable to stop herself. 'And this…this is my home.'

Lady Avery gave a shrill laugh. 'I don't think so. Why don't you go running to your boyfriend and ask if he wants you over the holiday period? *Because it's not going to happen, that's why.* Salvio will have moved on to the kind of women he's more usually associated with by now.' Her pale eyes drilled into Molly. 'Do you know, they say there isn't a supermodel on the planet he hasn't dated?'

'But why…why wait until now?' questioned Molly in a low voice. 'Why didn't you just fire me straight away?'

'With wall-to-wall engagements planned and Christmas just over the horizon?' Lady Avery looked at her incredulously. 'I was hardly going to dispense with your services and leave myself without a housekeeper at such a busy time, now, was I? That's what's known as cutting off your nose to spite your face.' There was a pause. 'You'll find you've been paid up to the end of the month, which is more generous than you deserve. Philip and I have decided to fly to Barbados tomorrow for a last-minute holiday and we're going out for the rest of the day. Just make sure you're gone by the time we return, will you, Molly?'

'But…but where will I go tonight?'

'You really think I care? There's a cheap B&B in the village. You can go there—*if* they'll take you.' Lady Avery's mouth had curved into a cruel smile. 'Just make sure you leave your car and house keys on the hall table before you go.'

And that was that. Molly could hardly believe it was happening. Except that she could. Her heart clenched as her old friend Fear re-entered her life without fanfare and suddenly she was back in that familiar situation of being in a fix. Only this time she couldn't blame her brother, or the vagaries of fate which had made her mother so ill throughout her childhood. This time it was all down to her.

Biting her lip, she thought desperately about where she could go and what she could do, but no instant solution sprang to mind. She had no relatives. No local friends who could provide her with a roof over her head until she found herself another live-in job. Her mind buzzed frantically as some of Lady Avery's words came flooding into her mind. How would Salvio react if she called him up and told him she'd been fired as a result of their crazy liaison? Would he do the decent thing and offer her a place to stay? Yet, despite recoiling at the thought of throwing herself on the mercy of a man who'd made it clear he wanted nothing but a one-night stand, it was growing increasingly clear that she might *have* to. Because the second bombshell was hovering overhead ready to explode, no matter how hard she tried to block it from her mind.

Telling herself it was stress which had made her period so late, she pushed the thought away as she remembered the card Salvio had given her—the one with a direct line to his assistant. What had he said? That his assistant knew plenty of people and could help her find a domestic role if ever she needed one. Molly licked her lips. She didn't want to do it but what choice did she have? Where would she even *start* looking for a new job and a home at this time of year?

Quickly, she packed her clothes, trying not to give in to the tears which were pricking at the backs of her eyes. Carefully she wedged in the framed photo of her mother and the one of Robbie in his school uniform, the cute image giving no hint of the gimlet-eyed teenager he would become. And only when she was standing in her threadbare winter coat, with a hand-knitted scarf knotted tightly around her neck, did she dial the number on the card with a shaking finger.

Salvio's assistant was called Gina and she didn't just sound friendly—she sounded *relieved* when Molly gave her name and explained why she was ringing.

'I can't believe it,' she said fervently. '*You* are the answer to my prayers, Molly Miller.'

'Me?' said Molly doubtfully.

'Yes, you.' Gina's voice softened. 'Are you free now? I mean, as of right now?'

'I am,' answered Molly cautiously. 'Why?'

'Because Salvio is having his annual pre-Christmas party in the Cotswolds tomorrow, just before he flies to Naples—and the housekeeper we'd hired has called to say her mother has fallen downstairs and broken her wrist, and she's had to cancel. If you can step in and take over at the last minute I can make it very worth your while.'

Molly pushed out the words from between suddenly frozen lips. 'That's very bad news—about the broken wrist, I mean, but I don't think I—'

But the tycoon's assistant was breezing on as if she hadn't spoken.

'Salvio must rate you very highly to have given you my number,' Gina continued. 'Why, it's almost like fate. I won't even have to bother telling him about the change. He doesn't like to be bogged down with domestic trivia and he's always so busy.'

Molly bit her lip so hard it hurt. This was fast becoming a nightmare, but what else could she do? How could she possibly turn down this opportunity just because she'd had sex with the man who would now unwittingly be employing her? She would just blend into the background and pray that the Neapolitan tycoon would be too busying partying to pay her any attention. And if the worst came to the worst and he discovered her identity—then she would shrug her shoulders and tell him it was no big deal.

Realistically, what could go wrong?

But being rumbled by Salvio wasn't the worst thing which could happen, was it? Not by a long way. The fear which had been nagging at her for days came flooding into her mind and this time would not be silenced, because all her excuses about stress and anxiety were rapidly fading. Because she wasn't sure if anxiety was capable of making your breasts ache and feel much bigger than usual. Or whether it could sap your normally voracious appetite.

She stared at her pale reflection in the hall mirror and saw the terror written in her own eyes. Because what if she was pregnant with Salvio De Gennaro's baby?

CHAPTER FIVE

VISIBILITY WAS POOR—in fact, it was almost non-existent. Salvio's fingers tightened around the soft leather of the steering wheel. Eyes narrowed, he stared straight ahead but all he could see was an all-enveloping whiteness swirling in front of the car windscreen. Every couple of seconds, the wipers dispelled the thick layer of snow which had settled, only to be rapidly replaced by another.

Frustrated, he glanced at the gold watch at his wrist, cursing the unpredictability of the weather. His journey from central London to the Cotswold countryside had been excruciatingly slow and in an ideal world he would have cancelled his annual party. But you couldn't really cancel something this close to Christmas, no matter how preoccupied you were feeling. And he *was* feeling preoccupied, no doubt about it—even though the reason for that was disconcertingly bizarre. An impatient sigh escaped his lungs as he watched another flurry of snow. Because he couldn't stop thinking about the curvy little housekeeper with the big grey eyes, with those luscious breasts, whose tips had fitted perfectly into his hungry mouth. Most of all, he couldn't stop remembering her purity. Her innocence.

Which he had taken. Without thought. Without knowledge. But certainly not without feeling.

Memories of how it had felt to penetrate her beautiful tightness flooded his mind and Salvio swallowed as he touched his foot against the brake pedal. Would he have bedded her so willingly if he'd known she was a virgin? Of course he wouldn't. His desire for the housekeeper had been completely out of character and he still couldn't quite fathom it. He usually enjoyed women who were, if not quite his equal, then certainly closer on the social scale than Molly Miller would ever be.

He thought about Beatriz—the Brazilian beauty with whom he'd been enjoying a long-distance flirtation for the past few months. He had been attracted to her because she'd played hard to get and he'd convinced himself that a woman who wouldn't tumble straight into his arms was exactly what he needed. But as her attitude towards him had thawed, so had his interest waned— and the memory of Molly had completely wiped her from his mind. And although Beatriz had made it clear she would be happy to share his bed after his Christmas party, the idea had left him cold, despite the fact that most men lusted after her statuesque beauty. He had been wondering about the most tactful way to convey his sudden change of heart, when she'd rung last night to say her plane had been delayed in Honolulu and she didn't think she was going to make his party. And hadn't he been struck by an overwhelming feeling of *relief*?

'*No importa.* Don't worry about it,' he had responded quickly—probably too quickly.

A pause. 'But I'm hoping we can see each other some other time, Salvio.'

'I'm hoping so too, but I'm flying out to Naples for Christmas and I'm not sure when I'll be back.' His response had been smooth and seasoned. And distinctly dismissive. 'I'll call you.'

He could tell from her sharp intake of breath that she understood the underlying message and her good-bye had been clipped and cold. She hadn't even wished him a happy Christmas and he supposed he couldn't blame her.

But his mind had soon moved on to other things and, infuriatingly, he kept recalling the sweet sensation of a naked Molly in his arms. He swallowed. The way her soft lips had pressed into his neck and her fleshy thighs had opened so accommodatingly. There were a million reasons why he shouldn't be thinking about her but she was proving a distractingly difficult image to shift. Was that because she hadn't put any demands on him? Because she'd been okay about him walking out of her life? Most women hung on in there, but Molly Miller was not among their number. And hadn't that intrigued him? Made him wonder what it might be like to see her in a more normal setting. Perhaps even take her out to dinner to see how long it would take for her allure to fade.

He'd thought a few times about contacting her—but what could he say, without falsely raising her hopes? No. He was doing her a favour by leaving her alone—

that was what he needed to remember. Breaking hearts was his default mechanism—and no way would he wish that kind of pain on the passionate little housekeeper.

It was the most beautiful house Molly had ever seen. Pressing her nose against the icy-cold glass, she peered out through the taxi window at the sprawling manor house, whose gardens were a clever combination of wild and formal and seemed to go on for ever. Although the sky was pewter-grey, the light was bright with snow and everything was covered in white. Fat flakes tumbled like giant feathers from the sky, so that the scene in front of her looked like one of those old-fashioned Christmas cards you couldn't seem to buy any more.

But Molly's emotions were in turmoil as the cab inched its way up the snowy drive. She had underestimated the impact of leaving Cornwall because even though the job had left a lot to be desired, it had still been her home and her security for the last two years. More than that, her departure had been forced upon her in the most dramatic and shameful of ways. Suddenly she felt rudderless—like a leaf caught up by a gust of wind being swirled towards an unknown destination.

But even worse than her near-homelessness was the confirmation of her worst fears. That it hadn't been stress or anxiety which had made her period so late. That the weird tugs of mood and emotion—like wanting to burst into tears or go to sleep at the most inopportune times—hadn't been down to the *worry* of getting pregnant. She couldn't even blame the sudden shock of losing her live-in job, or the corresponding jolt to her confidence. No, the reason had been made perfectly clear when she'd done not one, but two pregnancy tests in the overcrowded bathroom of the little boarding house she'd stayed in last night. With growing horror and a kind of numb disbelief she had sat back on her heels and stared at the unmistakable blue line, shaking with the shock of realising that she was pregnant with Salvio's baby.

And wondering what the hell she was going to do about it.

But she couldn't afford to think about that right now. The only thing she needed to concentrate on was doing her job—and as good a job as possible. She was going to have to tell him, yes, but not yet. Not right before his party and the arrival of his presumably high-powered guests.

She paid the driver and stepped out of the cab onto a soft blanket of snow. There were no other tyre marks on the drive and the only sign of life was a little robin hopping around as she made her way to the ancient oak front door, which looked like something out of a fairy tale. She knocked loudly, just in case—but there was no answer and so she let herself in with the keys she'd picked up from Salvio's assistant, along with a great big wodge of cash for expenses.

Inside, everything was silent except for the loud ticking of a grandfather clock, which echoed through the spacious hallway, and the interior was even more beautiful than the outside had suggested. It spoke of elegance and money and taste. Gleaming panelled walls carved with acorns and unicorns. Huge marble fireplaces and dark floorboards scattered with silk rugs were illuminated by the sharp blue light which filtered in through the windows. Yet the beauty and the splendour were wasted on Molly. She felt like an outsider. Like the spectre who had arrived at the feast bearing a terrible secret nobody would want to hear. She felt like curling up in a ball and howling, but what was the point of that? Instead she forced herself to walk around the house to get her bearings, just as she would with any new job.

A quick tour reassured her that the cupboards and fridge were well stocked with everything she could possibly need, the beds all made up with fresh linen and the fires laid. She lit the fires, washed her hands and started working her way through the to-do list. Barring bad weather cancellations, twenty-five guests would be arriving at seven. Gina had informed her that there were plenty of bedrooms if bad weather prevented some of the city guests getting back to London, but Salvio would prefer it if they left.

'He's a man who likes his own company,' she'd said.

'Does he?' Molly had questioned nervously, as an image shot into her head of a crying baby. How would he ever be able to deal with *that*?

Maybe he wouldn't want to.

Maybe he would tell her that he had no desire for an unplanned baby in his life. Had she thought about *that*?

A local catering company were providing a hot-buffet supper at around nine and wine waiters would take care of the drinks. All Molly had to do was make sure everything ran smoothly and supervise the local wait-

resses who were being ferried in from the nearby village. How difficult could it be? Her gaze scanned down
to the bottom of the list.

*And please don't forget to decorate the Christ-
mas tree!*

Molly had seen the tree the moment she'd walked
in—a giant beast of a conifer whose tip almost touched
the tall ceiling, beside which were stacked piles of card-
board boxes. Opening one, she discovered neat rows
of glittering baubles—brand-new and obviously very
expensive. And suddenly she found herself thinking
about Christmases past. About the little pine tree she
and Robbie used to drag in from the garden every year,
and the hand-made decorations which their mother had
knitted before the cruel illness robbed her of the ability to do even that. It had been hard for all of them to
watch her fading away but especially tough for her little
brother, who had refused to believe his beloved mother
was going to die. And Molly hadn't been able to do anything to stop it, had she? It had been her first lesson in
powerlessness. Of realising that sometimes you had to
sit back and watch awful things happen—and that for
once she couldn't protect the little boy she'd spent her
life protecting.

Didn't she feel that same sense of powerlessness now
as she thought of the cells multiplying in her womb?
Knowing that outwardly she looked exactly the same
as before, while inside she was carrying the Neapolitan's baby.

Her fingers were trembling as she draped the tree with fairy lights and hung the first bauble—watching it spin in the fractured light from the mullioned window. And then it happened—right out of nowhere, although if she'd thought about it she should have been expecting it. If she hadn't been singing 'In The Bleak Midwinter' at the top of her voice she might have heard the front door slam, or registered the momentary pause which followed. But she wasn't aware of anything until something alerted her to the fact that someone else was in the room. Slowly she turned her head to see Salvio standing there.

Her heart clenched tightly and then began to pound. He was wearing a dark cashmere overcoat over faded jeans and snowflakes were melting in the luxuriant blackness of his hair. She thought how tall and how powerful he looked. How his muscular physique dominated the space around him. All these thoughts registered in the back of her mind but the one which was at the forefront was the expression of disbelief darkening his olive-skinned features.

'You,' he said, staring at her from between narrowed eyes.

Molly wondered if the shock of seeing her had made him forget her name, or whether he had forgotten it anyway. In either case, he needed reminding—or this situation could prove even more embarrassing than it was already threatening to be. 'Yes, me,' she echoed, her throat dry with nerves. 'Molly. Molly Miller.'

'I know your name!' he snapped, in a way which made her wonder if perhaps he was protesting too much. 'What I want to know is what the hell you're doing here.'

His face had hardened with suspicion. It certainly wasn't the ecstatic greeting Molly might have hoped for—if she'd dared to hope for anything. But hope was a waste of time—she'd learnt that a long time ago. And at least a life spent working as a servant and having to keep her emotions hidden meant she was able to present a face which was perfectly calm. The only outward sign of her embarrassment was the hot colour which came rushing into her cheeks, making her think how unattractive she must look with her apron digging into her waist and her hair spilling untidily out of its ponytail. 'I'm just decorating the Christmas tree—'

'I can see that for myself,' he interrupted impatiently. 'I want to know *why*. What are you doing here, Molly?'

The accusation which had made his mouth twist with anger was unmistakable and Molly stiffened. Did he think she was stalking him, like one of those crazed ex-lovers who sometimes featured in the tabloids? Women who had, against all the odds, come into contact with a wealthy man and then been reluctant to let him—or the lifestyle—go.

'You gave me your assistant's card, remember?' she reminded him. 'And told me to ring her if I needed to find work.'

'But you already have a job,' he pointed out. 'You work for the Averys.'

Molly shook her head and found herself wishing she didn't have to say this. Because wasn't it a humiliating thing to have to admit—that she had been kicked out of her job just before Christmas? 'Not any more, I don't,' she said. She met the question which was glittering from his black eyes. 'Lady Avery caught me leaving your bedroom.'

His eyes narrowed. 'And she *sacked* you because of that?'

Molly's colour increased. 'I'm afraid so.'

Beneath his breath, Salvio uttered some of the words he'd learnt in the backstreets of Naples during his poverty-stricken childhood. Words he hadn't spoken in a long time but which seemed appropriate now as remorse clawed at his gut. It was his fault. Of course it was. Was that why she was looking at him with those big grey eyes, like some wounded animal you discovered hiding in the woods? Because she blamed him and held him responsible for what had happened? And it never *should* have happened, he told himself bitterly. He should never have invited her into his room for a drink, despite the fact that she'd been crying. He'd tried very hard to justify his actions. He'd told himself he'd been motivated by compassion rather than lust, but perhaps he had been deluding himself. Because ultimately he was a man and she was a woman and the chemistry between them had been as powerful as anything he'd ever experienced. Surely he wasn't going to deny *that*.

His eyes narrowed as he studied her. Despite her initial innocence, had she subsequently recognised the sexual power she had wielded over him? It wasn't inconceivable that her sacking had come about as a result of her own ego. She might easily have made a big show of leaving his room, with that dreamy look of sexual satisfaction which made a woman look more beautiful than fancy clothes ever could. And mightn't that have provoked Sarah Avery, whose advances he had most definitely rejected?

Suddenly he felt as if he was back on familiar territory, as he recalled the behaviour of women during his playing days, and one woman in particular. He remembered the dollar signs which had lit up in their eyes when they'd realised how much his contract had been worth. These days he might no longer be one of Italy's best-paid sportsmen, but in reality he was even wealthier. Was that why Molly Miller was here—prettily decorating his tree—just waiting to hit him with some kind of clumsy demand for recompense?

'So why exactly did Gina offer you this job?' he questioned.

She bit her lip. 'Because the woman who was supposed to be doing it had to suddenly go and look after her mother. And I didn't let on that I...' Her words faltered. 'That I *knew* you, if that's what you're worried about. Gina doesn't have a clue about what went on between us. There was a slot to fill, that's all—and I just happened to be in the right place at the right time.'

Or the wrong place at the wrong time. Just like the last time they'd met.

The thoughts rushed into Salvio's head before he could stop them and he felt his body tense as he worked out how best to handle this. Because now he found himself in a difficult situation. He frowned. The amazing night he'd shared with her had haunted him ever since, but nobody was going to deny that it had been a fool-hardy action on so many levels. Did she think it was going to happen again? he wondered. Was she expecting to resume her position in his bed? That once all his guests had left, he would be introducing her to another night of bliss?

He raked his gaze over her, unable to suppress the hunger which instantly fired up his blood but resenting it all the same. He shouldn't feel this way about her. He shouldn't still want her. That night had been a mistake and one which definitely shouldn't be repeated. Yet desire was spiralling up inside him with an intensity which took him by surprise and despite his best efforts he was failing to dampen it. With her fleshy curves accentuated by the waistband of an apron, she looked the antithesis of the glamour he'd always regarded as a prerequisite for his lovers. She looked *wholesome* and plain and yet somehow incredibly sexy.

Suddenly he felt a powerful urge to take her in his arms and lie her down beside the Christmas tree. To pull down her mismatched panties and kiss between those generous thighs, before losing his tongue and then his body in all that tight, molten heat. He wondered how she would react if he did. With the same breathtaking eagerness she had shown before—or would she push him away this time? His mouth hardened and so uncomfortably did his groin and, although he was unbearably tempted to test out the idea, he drew himself up, wondering if he'd taken leave of his senses.

He was her boss, for heaven's sake!

Shaking his head, he walked over to the window and

stared out at the thick white layer which was coating the lawns and bare branches of the trees. The light was fading from the sky, intensifying the monochrome colours of the garden so that all he noticed was the diamond-bright glitter of the ice-encrusted snow.

His mouth hardened. He'd thought tonight would just be another evening to get through, before flying out to Naples for a family Christmas. Slowly, he turned around. But suddenly everything had changed—and all because of this pink-faced woman who was standing in front of him, nervously chewing her lip.

'How long are you supposed to be working here?' he demanded.

'Just for tonight. And tomorrow I have to supervise the clean-up after the party.'

'And after that?' he probed. 'What then?'

She rubbed the tip of her ugly shoe over the Persian rug as if she were polishing it. 'I don't know yet. I'll just have to find something else.'

'Including accommodation, I suppose?'

She moved her shoulders awkwardly, as if he had reminded her of something she would prefer to forget, and when she looked up, her grey eyes were almost defiant. 'Well, yes. The jobs I take are always live-in.'

His eyes narrowed. 'And how easy will that be?'

Her attempt to look nonchalant failed and for the first time Salvio saw a trace of vulnerability on her face.

'Not very easy at this time of the year, I imagine.'

Salvio felt the flicker of a heavy pulse at his temple as another unwanted streak of conscience hit him and he recognised he couldn't just abandon her to the wolves.

He had bedded her and she had lost her job as a result of that—so it stood to reason he must take some of the responsibility. He nodded. 'Very well. Tomorrow, I'll have a word with Gina. See if we can't find you something more permanent.' He saw her face brighten and wondered if he had falsely raised her hopes. 'Not with me, of course,' he continued hastily. 'That isn't going to happen. The night we shared was many things, Molly, but it certainly didn't lay down a suitable foundation for any kind of working relationship between us.'

Molly flinched. She had thought him kind and that his behaviour towards her in the past had been thoughtful. But he wasn't kind, not really. He'd made it clear she couldn't ever work for him, not now she had been his lover—so, in effect, wasn't he patronising her just as much as Lady Avery had done? Before she thought she'd seen consideration in his face but that had been replaced by a flinty kind of calculation. Because Salvio De Gennaro could be utterly ruthless, she recognised— her heart sinking as she tried to imagine how he was going to react to her unwelcome news.

'Do you understand what I'm saying, Molly?' he continued remorselessly.

'Of course I do,' she said. 'I wasn't expecting to get a job with you. So please don't worry about it, Salv— Signor De Gennaro,' she amended, unable to hide her sudden flash of sarcasm. 'I won't bother you. You won't even know I'm here.'

The look on his face told her he didn't believe her and, despite her inexperience, Molly could understand why. Because how could they remain indifferent to each other when the atmosphere around them was still charged with that potent chemistry which had led to her downfall before? And wasn't she longing for him to touch her again? To trace his fingertip along the edges of her trembling lips, before replacing them with his mouth and kissing her until she capitulated to his every need.

Well, that would be insane.

Molly swallowed as she picked another bauble from its soft nest of tissue paper and the Neapolitan turned away.

'I need to get showered and changed before the party,' he said roughly. 'Just get on with your work, will you, Molly?'

CHAPTER SIX

SHE WISHED HE would stop staring at her.

Liar. Molly shivered as she picked up an empty wine glass and put it on her tray. *Admit it. You like it when he stares at you. Even though his face looks all dark and savage, as if he hates himself for doing it.*

And how much more savage will he look when he discovers the truth? she wondered.

It was the end of a long evening and only a few die-hard guests remained. Contrary to predictions the snow had stopped falling, allowing the chauffeur-driven cars to take the giggling London guests safely back to the capital. Vintage champagne had flowed, delicious food had been eaten and there hadn't been a single crisis in the kitchen, much to Molly's relief. A group of local singers had trudged through the snow and treated the partygoers to an emotional medley of Christmas carols, before being given mulled wine and hot mince pies and sent on their way with a huge donation to rebuild the roof of the village hall. And now Salvio was standing talking to a dark-suited man in the far corner of the huge drawing room—someone had whispered that he was a sheikh—but every time she looked up, Molly could see the hooded black eyes of the Neapolitan trained on her.

She hurried down to the kitchen where at least she was safe from that devastating gaze and the ongoing concern of how exactly she was going to break her momentous news. At least when you were helping stack clean plates and showing the hired help where to put all the silver cutlery, it was easy to forget your own problems, if only for a while. But at twenty past midnight the last of the staff departed and only the sheikh who had dominated Salvio's company for much of the evening was left, the two men deep in conversation as they sat by the fireside.

Molly was in the basement kitchen drying the final crystal glass when she heard a deafening chatter outside and peered out to see a helicopter alighting on the snowy lawn. Moments later the sheikh, now swathed in a dark overcoat, his black head bent against the flattening wind, began to run towards it. She could see the glint of a royal crest on the side of the craft as the door closed and it began its swaying ascent into the sky. Her hands were shaking as she suddenly realised she was alone in the house with Salvio and she wondered what she should do. She put the glass down. She should behave as she normally would in these circumstances— even if this felt anything like normal.

Taking off her damp apron and smoothing down her black dress, she went upstairs to find Salvio still sitting beside the fire, his stance fixed and unmoving as he gazed into the flickering flames. His long legs were stretched out before him and the rugged perfection of his profile looked coppery in the firelight. Never had he seemed more devastating or more remote and never had she felt so humble and disconnected. How crazy was it that this man had briefly been her lover and would soon be the father of her child?

Molly cleared her throat. 'Excuse me.'

He looked up then, his eyes narrowing as if he couldn't quite remember who she was, or why she was here.

'*Sì*, what is it?' he questioned abruptly.

'I didn't mean to disturb you, but I wondered if there was anything else you'd like?'

Salvio felt his heart slam hard against his chest. If it had been any other former lover asking that question, it would have been coated in innuendo. But Molly's words weren't delivered suggestively, or provocatively. Her big grey eyes weren't slanting out an unspoken invitation. She simply looked anxious to please, which only reinforced the differences between them. Once again he cursed his hot-headedness in taking the curvy housekeeper to his bed.

Even though he could understand exactly why he'd done it.

He'd spent this evening watching her, despite his best intentions. He'd told himself she was strictly off-limits and he should concentrate on his guests, but it had been Molly's wide-hipped sway which had captured his gaze and Molly's determined face as she had scurried around with trays of drinks and food which had captivated his imagination. He had seen the natural sparkle of her grey eyes and had remembered the healthy glow of her cheeks when she had romped enthusiastically in his arms. But her face was pale now, he noted. Deathly pale—as if all the colour had been leeched from it.

'No, I don't think there is,' he said slowly, forcing himself to treat her as he would any other member of staff. 'Thank you for all your hard work tonight, Molly. The party went very well. Even the Sheikh of Razrastan stayed far longer than he intended.'

'You're very welcome,' she said.

'I'm sure we can think about a generous bonus for you.'

'There's no need for that,' she said stiffly.

'I think I'll be the judge of that.' He gave her a benign smile. 'And I haven't forgotten my promise to try to find you some work. Or, rather, to ask Gina to help.' His words were tantamount to dismissal but she didn't move. Salvio saw the faint criss-crossing of a frown over the smooth expanse of her brow and something— he never knew what it was—compelled him to ask a question he usually avoided like the plague. 'Is everything okay?'

Her hands began twisting at the plain fabric of her work dress and he could see the indecision which made her frown deepen.

'Y-yes.'

'You don't sound very sure.'

'I wasn't going to tell you until tomorrow,' she said, her knuckles whitening.

Instinct made Salvio sit upright, his body tensing. 'Tell me *what*?' he questioned dangerously.

Molly licked her lips. She'd thought that a good night's

sleep and the addition of daylight might take some of the emotional sting out of her disclosure. But now she could see that any idea of sleep was a non-starter, especially with the thought of Salvio in bed nearby and the heavy realisation that he'd only ever wanted her that one time. But more than that, the news was bubbling inside her, wanting to get out. She needed to tell someone—and who else was she going to confide in?

'I'm pregnant,' she said bluntly.

There was a moment of silence—a weird and intense kind of silence. It was as if every sound in the room had been amplified to an almost deafening level. The crackle and spit of the fire. The loud thunder of her heart. The sudden intake of her own shuddered breath. And now there was shadow too, as Salvio rose from his chair—tall and intimidating—his powerful frame blocking out the firelight and seeming to fill the room with darkness.

'You can't be,' he said flatly. 'That is, if you're trying to tell me it's mine?'

She met the unyielding expression which had hardened his face and Molly's heart contracted with pain. Did he really think she'd lost her virginity to him and then rushed out to find herself another lover—as if trying to make up for lost time? Or was he just trying to run from his own responsibility? She stared at him reproachfully. 'You know it is.'

'I used contraception,' he bit out. 'You know I did.'

She felt blood rush into her cheeks. 'Maybe you weren't—'

'Careful?' He cut across her words with a bitter

laugh. 'I think that's a given, don't you? Reckless might be closer to the mark. On all counts.'

'Don't,' she said quickly.

His eyebrows shot up imperiously, as if he couldn't quite believe she was telling him what to do. *'What?'*

'Please don't,' she whispered. 'Don't make it any worse than it already is by saying things which will be difficult to forget afterwards.'

His eyes narrowed but he nodded, as if acknowledging the sense of her words. 'Are you sure?' he demanded. 'Or is it just a fear?'

She shook her head. 'I'm certain. I did a test.'

Another silence. 'I see.'

Molly's lips were dry and her heart was racing. 'I just want to make it clear that I'm only telling you because I feel duty-bound to tell you.'

'And not because you're after a slice of my fortune?'

Hurt now, she stared at him. 'You think that's what this is all about?'

His lips curved. 'Is it such a bizarre conclusion? Think about it, *mia bedda.* I'm rich and you're poor. What is it they say in the States?' He flicked the fingers of both hands, miming the sudden spill of money from a cash register. 'Ker-*ching!*'

Molly made to move away but his reflexes were lightning-fast and quicker than hers. He reached out to curl his fingers around her arm before pulling her towards him, like an expert angler reeling in their catch of the day. The movement made her breathless but it also made her hungry for him in a way she didn't want to be. Just one touch and her senses had started jangling, as she felt that now familiar desire washing over her. Meeting the gleam of his black eyes, she prayed she would find the strength to pull away from him and resist him. 'What do you think you're doing?' she demanded.

'I'm doing about the only thing which could possibly make me feel good right now,' he grated and brought his mouth down hard on hers.

Molly willed herself not to respond. She didn't have to do this—especially not after those insults he'd just hurled her way, making out she was some kind of gold-digger. But the trouble was that she *wanted* to kiss him. She wanted that more than anything else in the world right then. It was as if the beauty of his touch was making her realise how she'd got herself into this predicament in the first place. His kiss had been the first step to seduction and even now she found it irresistible. Closing her eyes, she let him plunder her lips until there was no oxygen left in her lungs and she had to draw back to suck in a breath of air. She shook her head distractedly. 'Salvio,' she whispered, but he shook his head.

'Don't say anything,' he warned, before scooping her up in his arms and carrying her out of the room.

Molly blinked in confusion because his hands were underneath her bottom and they were caressing it in a way which was making her want to squirm. As if in some kind of unbelievable dream he was carrying her up that sweeping staircase as if she were Scarlett O'Hara and he were Rhett Butler. And she was letting him.

So stop him. Make him put you down.

But she couldn't. Because *this* was powerlessness,

she realised—this feeling of breathy expectation bubbling up inside her as he kicked open the door of the master bedroom. The heavy oak door swung open as if it had been made of matchsticks as he carried her effortlessly across silken Persian rugs before depositing her on the huge bed.

And even though Molly could see no real affection on his proud Neapolitan features—nothing but sexual hunger glittering from his dark eyes—that didn't stop her from reciprocating. Was it the delicious memory of his lovemaking which made her open her arms to him and close them around him tightly? Or was it more basic than that? As he peeled her dress, shoes and underclothes from her body before impatiently removing his own clothes she began to wonder if there was some deep-rooted need to connect physically with the man whose seed was multiplying inside her.

Or at least, that was her excuse for what was about to happen.

'Salvio,' she gasped as his finger stroked a slow circle around the exquisitely aroused peak of her now bare nipple. *'Oh!'*

His naked body was warm against hers. 'Shh...'

It was more of a command than an entreaty but Molly heeded it all the same, terrified that words might break the spell and let reality flood in and destroy what she was feeling. His eyes were hooded as they surveyed her body, seeming to drink in every centimetre. Was she imagining his gaze lingering longest on her belly? With her notorious curves, she probably looked pregnant already. But now he was kissing her neck and her eyelids were fluttering to a close so that it became all about sensation rather than thought and that was so much better.

Encouraged by the hand now sliding from breast to thigh, Molly flickered her fingertips over the taut dip of his belly, her touch as delicate as if she were making pastry. And didn't his groan thrill her and fill her with a sense of pride that *she*—inexperienced Molly Miller—could make a man like Salvio react this way? Emboldened by his response, she drifted her hand over his rocky thighs, feeling the hair-roughened flesh turn instantly to goosebumps, and something about that galvanised him into action, because suddenly he was on top of her. He was kissing her with a hunger which was almost *ferocious* and, oh, it felt good. Better than anything had a right to feel. She could feel the graze of his jaw and his lips felt hard on hers, though his tongue was sinuous as it slipped inside her mouth.

She gave a little cry as she twisted restlessly beneath him and he gave a low laugh which was tinged with mockery.

'How quickly my little innocent becomes greedy,' he murmured. 'How quickly she has learnt what it is she wants.'

His words sounded more like insults than observations but by then he was stroking her wet and urgent heat and Molly was writhing beneath his fingers. She moaned as the sensation built and built and she realised what was about to happen. He was going to make her have an orgasm with his...*finger*.

'Salvio,' she cried out in disbelief, but just as she went tumbling over the top he thrust deep inside her.

She gasped as he filled her completely—even bigger than she remembered—and he gave a loud moan in response. And so did she. It felt as if her world were imploding. As if a jet-black sky had suddenly been punctured by a million stars. As if the two of them were locked and mingled for all time. Molly clung to him as she felt him momentarily stiffen before thrusting out his own shuddering pleasure.

He stayed inside her for countless minutes and Molly revelled in that sticky closeness because, in a funny sort of way, it felt as intimate as the act of sex had done. Maybe even more so, because now neither of them were chasing the satisfaction which had somehow left her feeling empty and satisfied, all at the same time.

But eventually he withdrew from her and rolled to the other side of the bed. Molly was careful to hide her disappointment as he threw the duvet over them both, quickly covering her up, as if the sight of her naked body offended him. She licked her lips as she waited for him to speak, planning to take her lead from him. It was the habit of a lifetime—of allowing her employer to dictate the conversation—because, technically, Salvio was still her employer, wasn't he? And it seemed vital that she stay quiet for long enough to hear his thoughts. Because what was said between them now was going to determine the rest of her baby's life, wasn't it? His attitude towards her unplanned pregnancy was of vital importance if they wanted to have any kind of amicable future. Not that she was expecting much from him. Not now. She'd thought she could rely on kindness until she'd realised she didn't really know him at all. And now her heart began to pound with anxiety as she wondered whether she should have given herself so easily to him. Could she really hope for respect in the circumstances?

She found herself studying him from between her lashes as she met the hard glitter of his eyes.

'So now what?' he questioned slowly.

She took him literally, because wasn't it simpler all round if she remained practical and continued to do her job? 'I ought to go down and turn off all the lights—especially the tree lights.'

His face was incredulous. 'Excuse me?'

She pushed her hair away from her face and wriggled into a sitting-up position, though she was careful to keep the top of the duvet modestly covering her breasts. 'I haven't switched off the lights on the Christmas tree—and there's also the fire, which we've left unguarded,' she said. 'I can't possibly go to sleep until all that is in place.'

'The fireguard?' he echoed disbelievingly, looking momentarily bemused before nodding. 'Wait here,' he said, and climbed out of bed.

Quite honestly, Molly didn't feel as if she had the strength or inclination to go anywhere—especially not when an unclothed Salvio was walking towards the door, seemingly unaware of the fact that it was the middle of winter and the snow was thick on the ground outside. She gazed at him as if hypnotised—her eyes drinking in the pale globes of his buttocks, which contrasted so vividly with the burnished olive of his thighs. And then he turned round, frowning with faint concern as he surveyed her, as if he had suddenly remembered that she'd just announced her pregnancy and wasn't quite sure how to deal with her any more.

'Can I get you anything?'

She guessed he was being literal too and that it would have been pointless to have asked for a crystal ball to re-assure her about her baby's future. And pointless to have asked for some affirmation that he wasn't planning on deserting his unplanned child, even if he wanted noth-ing more to do with her. But unlike her brother, Molly had never been a fantasist. She cleared her throat and nodded. 'A drink of water would be nice.'

She waited for him to say something like, *I'll bring it to your room*, but he didn't. Which presumably meant it was okay to stay here.

Of *course* it was okay to stay here—they'd just had sex, hadn't they?

But it wasn't easy to shrug off a lifetime of being deferential and Molly even felt slightly guilty about rushing into the luxurious en-suite bathroom and avail-ing herself of the upmarket facilities. She splashed her face with water and smoothed down her mussed hair before returning to the bed and burrowing down be-neath the duvet.

And then he was back and Molly quickly averted her eyes because the front view of the naked Neapoli-tan was much more daunting than the back had been—particularly as he seemed to be getting aroused again.

Did he read something in her expression? Was that why he gave a savage kind of laugh as he handed her the glass of water? 'Don't worry,' he grated. 'I'll endeavour to keep my appetite in check while we discuss how we're going to handle this.'

The large gulp of water she'd been taking nearly choked her and Molly put the glass down on the bedside table with a hand which was trembling. 'There's nothing to handle,' she said shakily. 'I'm having this baby, no matter what you say.'

'You think I would want anything other than that?' he demanded savagely.

'I wasn't… I wasn't sure.'

Salvio climbed into bed, disappointed yet strangely relieved that her magnificent breasts weren't on show, meaning he'd be able to concentrate on what he needed to say and not on how much he would like to lose himself in her sweet tightness again. He pulled the cover over the inconvenient hardening of his groin. Was she really as innocent as she seemed? Physically, yes—he had discovered that for himself. But was she really so unschooled in the ways of the world that she didn't realise that she was now in possession of what so many women strived for?

A billionaire father for her baby.

A meal ticket for life.

And there wasn't a damned thing he could do about it. Fate had thrown him a curveball and he was just going to have to deal with it.

'Tell me about yourself,' he said suddenly.

She blinked. 'Me?'

The sigh he gave wasn't exaggerated. 'Look, Molly— I think you're in danger of overplaying the wide-eyed innocent, don't you? We've had sex on a number of occasions and you've just informed me you're pregnant. Ordinarily I wouldn't be interested in hearing about your past, but you'll probably agree that this is no ordinary situation.'

Molly's heart clenched as his cruel words rained down on her. Wouldn't another man at least have *pretended* to be interested in what had made her the person she was today? Gone through some kind of polite ritual of getting to know her. Maybe she should be grateful that he hadn't. He might be cruel, but at least he wasn't a hypocrite. He wasn't pretending to feel stuff about her and building up her hopes to smash them down again. At least she knew where she stood.

'I was born in a little cottage—'

'Please. Spare me the violins. Let's just cut to the chase, shall we?' he interrupted coolly. 'Parents?'

Molly shrugged. 'My father left my mother when she was diagnosed with multiple sclerosis,' she said flatly.

She saw a flare of something she didn't recognise in his black eyes.

'That must have been hard,' he said softly.

'It was,' she conceded. 'Less so for me than for my little brother, Robbie. He...well, he adored our mother. So did I, obviously—but I was busy keeping on top of everything so that social services were happy to let me run the home.'

'And then?' he prompted, when her words died away.

Molly swallowed. 'Mum died when Robbie was twelve, but they let us carry on living together. Just me and him. I fought like crazy not to have him taken into care and I succeeded.'

His dark brows knitted together. 'And what was that like?'

She thought she detected a note of sympathy in his voice, or was that simply wishful thinking? Of course it was. He was cruel and ruthless, she reminded herself. He was only asking her these questions because he felt he *needed* to—not because he *wanted* to. For a moment Molly was tempted to gloss over the facts. To tell him that Robbie had turned out fine. But what if he found out the truth and then accused her of lying? Wouldn't that make this already difficult situation even worse than it already was?

'Robbie went off the rails a bit,' she admitted. 'He did what a lot of troubled teenagers do. Got in with the wrong crowd. Got into trouble with the police. And then he started...'

Her voice tailed off again, knowing this was something she couldn't just consign to the past. Because the counsellor had told her that addictions never really went away. They just sat there, brooding and waiting for someone to feed them. And wasn't she scared stiff that they were being fed right now—that someone was busy dealing cards across a light-washed table in the centre of a darkened room somewhere in the Outback?

'What did he start, Molly?' prompted Salvio softly.

'Gambling.' She stared down at her short, sensible fingernails before glancing up again to meet the ebony gleam of his eyes. 'It started off with fruit machines and then he met someone in the arcade who said a bright boy like him would probably be good at cards. That he could win enough money to buy the kind of things he'd never had. And that's when it all started.'

'*It?*'

Molly shrugged. 'I think Robbie was still missing Mum. I know he'd been frustrated and unhappy that we'd been so poor while she was alive. Whatever it was, he started playing poker and he was good at it. At first. He started winning money but he spent it just as quickly. More quickly than it was coming in. And the trouble with cards is that the more you want to win— the worse you become. They say that your opponent can smell desperation and Robbie was as desperate as hell. He started getting into debt. Big debt. But the banks didn't want to know and so he borrowed from some pay-day lenders and they...they...'

'They came after him?' Salvio finished grimly.

Molly nodded. 'I managed to use most of my savings to pay them off, though there's still an outstanding debt which never seems to go down because the interest rates they charge are astronomical. I wanted Robbie to have a fresh start. To get away from all the bad influences in his life. So he went to Australia to get the whole gambling bug out of his system and promised to attend Gamblers Anonymous. That's why I was working for the Averys. They were hardly ever in the house so I got to live there rent-free. Plus they paid me a lot of money to look after all their valuable artefacts. They said their insurance was lower if they had someone living permanently on the premises.'

'And then I came along,' he mused softly.

Molly's head jerked back as something in his tone alerted her to danger. 'I'm sorry?'

His bare shoulders gleamed like gold in the soft light from the lamp. 'A young attractive woman like you must have found it incredibly limiting to be shut away in that huge house in the middle of nowhere working for people who only appeared intermittently,' he observed. 'It must have seemed like a gilded prison.'

'I was grateful for a roof over my head and the chance to save,' she said.

'And the opportunity to meet a rich man who might make a useful lover?'

Molly's mouth fell open. 'Are you out of your mind?'

'I don't think so, *mia bedda*,' he contradicted silkily. 'I base my opinions on experience. It's one of the drawbacks of being wealthy and single—that women come at you from all angles. You must have acknowledged that I was attracted to you, and I can't help wondering whether you saw me as an easy way out of your dilemma. Were the bitter tears you cried real, or manufactured, I wonder? Did you intend those sobs to stir my conscience?'

Molly sat up in bed, her skin icy with goosebumps, despite the duvet which covered most of her naked body. 'You think I *pretended to cry*? That I deliberately got myself pregnant to get you to pay off my brother's debts? That I would cold-bloodedly use my baby as a bargaining tool?'

'No, I'm not saying that. But I do think that fate has played right into your hardworking little hands,' he said slowly. 'Don't you?'

Her voice was shaking as she shook her head. 'No. No, I don't.' Pushing the duvet away, she swung her legs over the side of the bed, acutely conscious of her wobbly bottom as she bent down and started pulling on her discarded clothes with fingers which were trembling, telling herself she would manage. Somehow. Because she had always managed before, hadn't she? Fully dressed now, Molly turned round, steeling herself not to react to his muscular olive body outlined so starkly against the snowy white bedding. 'There's nothing more to be said, is there?'

He gave a bitter laugh. 'Oh, I think there's plenty which needs to be said, but not tonight, not when emotions are running high. I need to think first before I come to any decision.'

Molly was tempted to tell him that maybe he should have done that before he had taken her to bed and then come out with a stream of unreasonable accusations, but what was the point in inflaming an already inflamed situation? And she couldn't really blame him for the sex, could she? Not when she had been complicit every step of the way. Not when she had desperately wanted him to touch her.

And the awful thing was that she still did.

Tilting her chin upwards and adopting the most dignified stance possible—which wasn't easy in the circumstances—she walked out of Salvio's bedroom without another word.

CHAPTER SEVEN

A COLD BLUE light filtered into the tiny bedroom, startling Molly from the bewildering landscape of unsettled sleep—one haunted by Salvio and the memory of his hard, thrusting body. Disorientated, she sat up in bed, wondering if she'd dreamt it all. Until the delicious aching at her breasts and soft throb between her legs reminded her that it had happened. Her heart began to race. It had actually happened. At the end of an evening's service she had informed her employer she was pregnant with his baby.

And had then been carried up the staircase and willingly had sex with him, despite all the things he'd accused her of.

Did he really believe it was his wealth which had attracted her to him, when she would have found him irresistible if he'd been covered in mud and sweat from working the fields?

Slowly, she got out of bed. She didn't know what Salvio wanted. All she knew was what *she* wanted. Her hand crept down to cover the soft flesh of her belly. She wanted this baby.

And nothing Salvio did or said was going to change her mind.

She showered and washed her hair—pulling on clean jeans and a jumper the colour of a winter sky before going downstairs, to be greeted by the aroma of coffee. In the kitchen she found Salvio pouring himself an inky cupful, and although he looked up as she walked in, his face registered no emotion. He merely gestured to the pot.

'Want some?'

She shook her head. 'No, thanks. I'll make myself some tea.' She was certain herbal tea was better for babies than super-strong coffee, but mainly she welcomed the opportunity of being able to busy herself with the kettle. Anything rather than having to confront the distracting vision of Salvio in faded jeans and a sweater as black as his hair. She could feel him watching her and she had to try very hard not to appear clumsy— no mean feat when that piercing gaze was trained on her like a bird of prey. But when she couldn't dunk her peppermint teabag a moment longer, she was forced to turn around and face him, glad he was now silhouetted against the window and his features were mostly in shadow.

'So,' he said, without preamble. 'We need to work out what we're going to do about the astonishing piece of news you dropped into my lap last night. Any ideas, Molly?'

Molly had thought about this a lot during those long hours when sleep had eluded her. *Be practical*, she urged herself. *Take the emotion out of it and think facts.*

She cleared her throat. 'Obviously finding a job is paramount,' she said cautiously. 'A live-in job, of course.'

'A live-in job,' he repeated slowly. 'And when the baby is born, what then?'

Molly hoped her shrug conveyed more confidence than she actually felt. 'Lots of people don't mind their staff having a baby around the place. Well, maybe not lots of people,' she amended when she heard his faintly incredulous snort and acknowledged that he might have a point. 'But houses which already have children tend to be more accommodating. Who knows? I might even switch my role from housekeeper to nanny.'

'And that's what you want, is it?'

Molly suppressed the frustration which had flared up inside her. Of course it wasn't. But she couldn't really tell him that none of this was what she *wanted*—not without betraying the child she carried. She hadn't planned to get pregnant, but she would make the best of it. Just as she hadn't planned for the father of her child to be a cold-hearted billionaire who right now felt so distant that he might as well have been on another planet, rather than standing on the other side of the kitchen. She wanted what most women wanted when they found themselves in this situation—a stable life and a man who adored them. 'Life is all about adaptation,' she said stolidly when, to her surprise, he nodded, walking away from the window and putting his coffee cup down on the table before pulling out a chair.

'I agree,' he said. 'Here. Sit down. We need to talk about this properly.'

She shook her head. 'I can't sit down.'

'Why not?'

'Because I still have to clear up the house, after the party.'

'Leave it.'

'I can't leave it, it's what you're paying me—'

'I said leave it, Molly,' he snapped. 'I can easily get people in to do that for me later. Just sit down, will you?'

Molly opened her mouth to refuse. To tell him that the walls felt as if they were closing in on her and his presence was making her jittery. But what else could she do? Flounce out into the snow, two days before Christmas Day—with nowhere to go and a child in her belly? Ignoring the chair he was holding out for her, she chose one at the opposite end of the table and sank down onto it, her mouth unsmiling as she looked at him questioningly.

'I've given a lot of thought to what's happened,' he said, without preamble.

Join the club. 'And did you come to any conclusions?'

Salvio's eyes narrowed as she stared at him suspiciously. She wasn't behaving as he had expected her to behave. Although what did he know? He'd never had to face something like this before and never with someone like her. After her departure last night, he'd thought she might try to creep back into his bed—maybe even whisper how sorry she was for flouncing out like that—before turning her lips to his for another hungry kiss. He was used to the inconsistency of women—and in truth he would have welcomed a reconnection with those amazing curves. Another bout of amazing sex might have given him a brief and welcome respite from his concerns about the future.

She hadn't done that, of course, and so he had braced himself for sulks or tears or reproachful looks when he bumped into her this morning. But no. Not that either. Sitting there in a soft sweater which matched her grey eyes, with her hair loose and shining around her shoulders, she looked the picture of health—despite the shadows beneath her eyes, which suggested her night had been as troubled as his.

And the crazy thing was that this morning he hadn't woken up feeling all the things he was expecting to feel. There had been residual shock, yes, but the thought of a baby hadn't filled him with horror. He might even have acknowledged the faint flicker of warmth in his heart as a tenuous glimmer of pleasure, if he hadn't been such a confirmed cynic.

'Every problem has a solution if you come at it from enough angles,' he said carefully. 'And I have a proposition to put to you.'

She creased her brow. 'You do?'

There was a pause. 'I don't want you finding a job as a housekeeper, or looking after someone else's children.'

'Why not?'

Salvio tensed, sensing the beginning of a negotiation. Was she testing out how much money he was prepared to give her? 'Isn't it obvious? Because you're pregnant with my baby.' His voice deepened. 'And although this is a child I never intended to have, I'm prepared to accept the consequences of my actions.'

'How…how cold-blooded you make it sound,' she breathed.

'Do you want me to candy-coat it for you, Molly?' he demanded. 'To tell you that this was what I always secretly dreamed would happen to me? Or would you prefer the truth?'

'I'm a realist, Salvio,' she answered. 'I've only ever wanted the truth.'

'Then here it is, in all its unvarnished glory. Tomorrow, I'm flying home to Naples for the holidays.'

'I know. Your assistant told me when she hired me.'

'I return every year,' he continued slowly. 'To two loving parents who wonder where they went so wrong with their only child.'

She blinked at him in confusion. 'I don't…understand.'

'Who wonder why their successful, handsome son who has achieved so much,' he continued, as if she hadn't spoken, 'has failed to bring home a woman who will one day provide them with the grandchildren they yearn for.' He gave a sudden bitter laugh. 'When, hey, what do you know? Suddenly I have found such a woman and already she is with child! What a gift it will be for them to meet you, Molly.'

She stared at him, confusion darkening her grey eyes. '*Meet* them? You're not suggesting—'

'Like I said last night—it's time to lose all that wide-eyed innocence. I think you know exactly what I'm suggesting,' he drawled. 'We buy you a big diamond ring and I take you home to Naples as my fiancée.'

'You mean…' She blinked. 'You mean you want to marry me?'

'Let's put it another way. I don't particularly want to marry anyone, the difference is that I'm *prepared* to marry you,' he amended.

'Because of the baby?'

'Because of the baby,' he agreed. 'But not just that. Most women are demanding and manipulative but, interestingly enough, you are none of those things. Not only are you extremely beddable—I find you exceptionally…*agreeable*.' His lips curved into a reflective smile. 'And at least you know your place.'

Molly stared at him, wanting to tell him to stop making her sound like the UK representative for the international society of doormats. Until she realised that once again Salvio was speaking the truth. She *did* know her place. She always had done. When you worked as a servant in other people's houses, that was what tended to happen.

'So what's in it for me?' she asked, thinking she ought to say *something*.

He looked at her in surprise. 'It isn't very difficult to work out. You get financial security and I get a ready-made family. I can pay off your brother's debt in one swoop, on the understanding that this is the only time I bankroll him. And if I were you, I would wipe the horror from your face, Molly. It really isn't a good look for a woman who's on the brink of getting engaged.' His voice dipped into one of silky admonishment. 'And it isn't as if you have a lot of choices, do you?'

Molly felt the sudden shiver of vulnerability rippling

down her spine. He didn't have to put it quite so brutally, did he? She swallowed. Or maybe he did. It was yet another cruel observation but it was true. She *didn't* have a lot of choices. She knew there was nothing romantic about having to struggle. She'd done all that making-the-best-of-a-bad-situation stuff—seeing how many meals you could get out of a bag of black-eyed beans and buying her clothes in thrift stores. She knew how hard poverty could be.

And this was her baby.

Her defenceless little *baby*.

She was aware of her hand touching her belly and aware of Salvio's gaze following the movement before he lifted his black eyes to hers. She searched their dark gleam in vain for some kind of emotion, and tried to ignore the painful stab in her heart when she met nothing but a cold, unblinking acceptance in their ebony depths. Of course he wasn't going to feel the same way as she did about their child. Why *wouldn't* he look sombre? Having his life inextricably linked to that of a humble little housekeeper was surely nothing for the Neapolitan billionaire to celebrate.

'Very well. Since—as you have already pointed out—I have very little alternative... I agree,' she said, and then, because subservience was as much a part of her life as breathing and because deep down she *was* grateful to him for his grudging generosity, she added a small smile. 'Thank you.'

Salvio felt his gut clench, knowing he didn't deserve her thanks. Or that shy look which made him want to cradle her in his arms. He knew he could have asked her to marry him in a more romantic way. He could have dropped onto one knee and told her he couldn't imagine life without her. But why get her used to an attitude he could never sustain and raise expectations which could never be met? The only way he could make this work was if he was straight with her, and that meant not making emotional promises he could never fulfil.

But he knew one sure way to please her—the universal way to every woman's heart. 'Go and get your stuff together, *nicuzza*,' he said softly. 'We're going shopping.'

Molly stepped out onto the icy Bond Street pavement feeling dazed but warm. Definitely warm. Who would have ever thought a coat could *be* so warm? Wonderingly she brushed her fingertips over the camel cashmere, which teamed so well with the knee-length boots and the matching brown leather gloves which were as soft as a second skin. She caught sight of her reflection in one of the huge windows of the upmarket department store and stared at it, startled—wondering if that glossy confection of a woman was really her.

'*Sì*, you look good,' Salvio murmured from beside her.

She looked up into his ruggedly handsome face. 'Do I?'

'Good enough to eat,' he affirmed, his black eyes glittering out an unspoken message and Molly could do nothing about the shiver which rippled down her spine and had nothing to do with the icy temperature.

After a slow drive through the snow to London, he

had brought her to one of the capital's most famous streets, studded with the kind of shops which were guarded by burly security men with inscrutable expressions. But the faces of the assistants inside were far more open and Molly knew she hadn't imagined the faint incredulity which greeted her appearance, as women fluttered around Salvio like wasps on a spill of jam.

He asked for—and got—a terrifyingly sleek stylist, who was assigned the daunting task of dressing her. Endless piles of clothing and lingerie were produced— some of which were instantly dismissed by an impatient wave of Salvio's hand and some of which were met with a slow smile of anticipation.

'It seems a silly amount of money to spend since whatever I buy isn't going to fit me for very long,' she hissed in a fierce undertone after nearly fainting when she caught sight of one of the price tags.

He seemed amused by her attempt to make economies. 'Then we'll just have to buy you some more, won't we? Don't worry about the cost, Molly. You will soon be the wife of a very wealthy man.'

It was hard to imagine, thought Molly as a feather-light chiffon dress floated down over her head, covering an embroidered bra whose matching panties were nothing more than a flimsy scrap of silk. As she appeared from behind the velvet curtain of the changing room to meet Salvio's assessing gaze, she began to wonder if he'd done this whole transformation thing before. And she wondered whether she should show a little pride and refuse all the gifts he was offering.

But then she thought about the reality. Salvio probably came from an extremely wealthy family who might not take kindly to someone from her kind of background. Wouldn't she feel even more out of place if she turned up looking like a poor relation in her cheap clothes and worn boots? Which was why she submitted to the purchase of sweaters and jeans, jackets and day dresses—and the most beautiful shoes she had ever seen. Gorgeous patent stilettos in three different colours, which somehow had the ability to add precious inches to her height and make her walk in a different and more feminine way.

And when they were all done and the glossy bags had been placed in the limousine which had been slowly tailing them, Salvio guided her past yet another security guard and into a jewellery shop where inside it was all light and dazzle. Locked glass cases contained the biggest diamonds Molly had ever seen—some the colour of straw, some which resembled pink champagne, and some even finer than Lady Avery's vast collection of family jewels.

'So what's your ideal ring? What did you used to dream about when you were a little girl?' asked Salvio softly, his fingers caressing the small of her back as an elegant saleswoman approached them. 'Whatever takes your fancy, it's yours.'

Did he have to put it quite like that? Molly wondered, moving away to avoid the distraction of his touch. The only thing she used to dream about when she was a little girl was making sure there was a hot meal on the table, and wondering if she'd managed to get all Mum's pills from the pharmacy. Yet Salvio was making her sound like someone whose gaze was bound to be riveted by the biggest and brightest ring in the shop.

She could feel her cheeks growing hot, because suddenly this felt like the charade it really was. As if they were going through all the motions of getting engaged, but with none of the joy or happiness which most couples would have experienced at such a time. And while Salvio's handsome face was undeniably sensual, his jet-dark eyes were as cold as any of the jewels on display. Molly lifted her gaze from the display cabinet as a quiet air of certainty ran through her. 'I don't want anything which looks like an engagement ring,' she said.

Hiding her surprise, the assistant produced a ring to just that specification—a stunning design of three thin platinum bands, each containing three asymmetrically placed diamonds which glittered and sparkled in the sharp December sunlight. 'The diamonds are supposed to resemble raindrops,' the young woman said gently.

Or tears, thought Molly suddenly. They looked exactly like tears.

From Bond Street they were whisked to Salvio's home in a fashionable area of London. Molly had heard of Clerkenwell but had never actually been there—just as she'd never been in such a gleaming, modern penthouse apartment before. She wandered from room to room. Everything was shiny and clean, but it was stark—as if nobody really lived there. It was as if some designer had been allowed to keep all décor to a minimum, but its sleek emptiness wasn't her main worry—which was that it was no place for a baby.

What was left of the day rushed past in a whirl of organisation but for once it wasn't Molly doing the organising, since Salvio seemed to have fleets of people at his disposal. People to organise cars and planes. To book hotels and arrange the last-minute purchase of gifts. They ate an early supper, which was delivered and served by staff from a nearby award-winning restaurant who even provided candles and a fragrant floral centrepiece.

'You don't have a chef, or a housekeeper?' Molly asked, as she sat down at the glass dining table and tried not to think about how dangerous a piece of furniture like this might be for a young child.

'I prefer to keep resident staff to a minimum. It optimises my privacy,' Salvio explained coolly, as two delicate soufflés were placed in front of them. 'I hope you're hungry?'

'Very,' she said, shaking out her napkin and trying not to dwell on what he'd just said about privacy—because he was about to have it shattered in the most spectacular way. 'Have you lived here for very long?' she questioned.

'I've had the apartment for about five years.'

'And you're here a lot?'

'No, not really. I have other homes all round the world. This is just my base whenever I'm in London.' He gazed at her thoughtfully. 'Why do you ask?'

She shrugged. 'It's very tidy.'

He laughed. 'I thought, given your occupation, that tidiness might meet with your approval.'

And oddly enough, that hurt. It was yet another reminder of just how far out of her comfort zone she was. A reminder of how he really saw her. She would never be his equal, she thought, as a powerful wave of fatigue washed over her.

'Actually, I'm pretty tired,' she said. 'It's a been a long day and the baby...'

The baby.

Salvio pushed away his wine glass. They hadn't mentioned it all afternoon but the word no longer hit him like a shock. He was slowly getting used to the idea that she was pregnant, even if he wasn't exactly jumping for joy about it. And Molly Miller was proving easier company than he had expected. Undemanding and optimistic. There was something about her quiet presence which made him feel almost *peaceful*. He stared at her washed-out face and felt an unexpected wave of remorse wash over him. Why hadn't he noticed how tired she might be?

'You need to go to bed,' he said resolutely, pushing back his chair.

He saw her throat constrict.

'Where...where am I sleeping?'

'We're supposed to be an engaged couple, Molly,' he said, almost gently. 'Where do you think you'll be sleeping?'

'I wasn't...sure.'

He'd assumed she would be sharing his bed, because why wouldn't he? But something about her pallor and trepidation made him reconsider—for his own sake as well as for hers. Wouldn't a night apart re-establish his habitual detachment—especially since it was obvious neither of them had slept well last night?

He rose to his feet. 'There's no need to sound so fearful, Molly,' he said. 'I'll show you the spare room. You'll have plenty of peace in there.'

He saw the sudden look of uncertainty which crossed her features and then she nodded her head, the way he'd seen her do before.

'That sounds like a good idea,' she said, with what sounded like obedience, and once again he was reminded of the fact that she was, essentially, a servant.

CHAPTER EIGHT

BATHED IN THE bright December sunshine which flooded in through the giant windows of their Neapolitan hotel suite, Molly turned to Salvio, who was just changing out of the jeans and leather jacket he'd worn for the trip over, into something a little more formal.

'We still haven't discussed—' Molly hesitated '—what we're going to tell your parents.'

Pausing in the act of straightening his tie, Salvio turned to look at his fiancée. She looked…incredible, he thought. With her shiny hair scooped on top of her head and her curvy shape encased in a dress the colour of spring leaves, there was no trace of that shy and frumpy housekeeper now. They'd just arrived in his home city— his jet descending through the mountains surrounding the mighty Mount Vesuvius, with all its unleashed power and terrible history. It was an iconic view which took away the breath of the most experienced traveller and he had found himself watching Molly for her reaction. But, oblivious to the beauty which surrounded them, she had seemed lost in thought. Even when the car had whisked them to this luxury hotel overlooking the Castel dell'Ovo and a lavish suite which even *he* could not fault, she seemed barely to register the opulence of their penthouse accommodation.

He wondered if she'd noticed the sideways stares he'd been receiving from the moment they'd stepped off the plane. The double takes and the *'Is it him?'* looks which were as familiar to him as breathing, whenever he returned to his native town. Yet Molly had been impervious to them all.

'We tell them the truth,' he said eventually, giving some thought to her question. 'That you're pregnant and we're getting married as soon as possible.'

She winced a little. 'Do you think we need to be quite so…?'

His gaze bored into her. 'So what, Molly?'

She licked her lips and, mesmerised by the resulting gleam which emphasised their soft beauty, Salvio momentarily cursed himself for not admitting her to his bed last night. Had he really imagined such an action might make him more detached and rational, when he'd been obsessing about her all night long?

'Brutal,' she concluded, pursing her lips together as if it wasn't a word she particularly wanted to use.

'Brutal?'

She shrugged and began walking across the room, pausing only to peer into the elevated stone hot tub which stood at the far end of the enormous suite—an extravagant touch eclipsed only by the tall decorated Christmas tree which was framed in one of the tall windows.

Eventually she came to a halt and perched on an orange velvet chair to look at him. 'You told me you're known as someone who is a commitment-phobe. Someone who doesn't want to get married,' she said.

Salvio gave his tie a final tug. That wasn't the whole story, but why burden her with stuff she didn't need to know? 'What of it?'

'So this sudden marriage is going to come as a bolt out of the blue to your parents, isn't it?'

'And?' he questioned coolly. 'Your point is?'

She studied her left hand warily, as if she couldn't quite get used to the diamond knuckle-duster she was wearing. 'I'd prefer not to say anything about my pregnancy—at least, not yet. It's still very early days. I just thought it might be nice if we could at least *allow* them to think it might be about more than just the unwanted fallout of a...a...'

Her words tailed away and Salvio wondered if, in her innocence, she simply didn't know all the expressions—some of them crude—she could have used to describe what had happened between them that first night. 'A hook-up?' he put in helpfully, before adopting a more caustic tone. 'Are you saying you want to pretend to my parents that this is some great kind of love affair?'

'Of course not.' She flushed before lifting a reproachful grey gaze to his. 'I don't think you're that good an actor, are you, Salvio?'

He inclined his head as if to concede the point. 'Or that good a liar?'

'That's another way of putting it, I suppose.'

He acknowledged her crestfallen expression. 'I don't want to raise your hopes, Molly—or theirs. It's just who I am. And the bottom line is I just don't do emotion. That's all.'

'That's…that's quite a lot,' she observed. 'Do you think…?' She seemed to choose her words very carefully. 'Do you think you were born that way?'

'I think circumstances made me that way,' he said flatly.

'What kind of circumstances?'

Salvio frowned. This was deeper than he wanted to go because he was a man with a natural aversion to the in-depth character analysis which was currently in vogue. But what had he imagined would happen—that he could take an innocent young girl as his wife and present to her the same impenetrable exterior which had made scores of women despair at his coldness in the past? He walked over to the drinks cabinet, ignoring the expensive bottles of wine on display, pouring instead two crystal glasses of mineral water before walking across the room to hand her one. 'You don't know much about me, do you, Molly?'

She shook her head as she sipped her drink. 'Practically nothing. How would I? We haven't exactly sat down and had long conversations since we met, have we?'

He almost smiled. 'You weren't tempted to go and look me up online?'

Molly didn't answer immediately as she met the scrutiny of his piercing black gaze. Of course she'd been *tempted*. Someone like Salvio was high profile enough to have left a significant footprint on the Internet, which she could have accessed at the touch of a computer key, and naturally she was curious about him. But she'd felt as if their lives were unequal enough already. The billionaire tycoon and the humble housekeeper. If she discovered stuff about him, would she then have to feign ignorance in the unlikely event that he wanted to confide in her? If she heard anything about him, she wanted to hear it *from* him—not through the judgemental prism of someone else's point of view.

'I didn't want to seem as if I was spying on you.'

'Very commendable.'

'But it would be useful to know,' she continued doggedly. 'Otherwise your parents might think we're nothing but strangers.'

'And is that what concerns you, Molly?' His black gaze continued to bore into her. 'What other people think?'

Molly bit back her instinctive response to his disdainful question. If she'd been bothered about things like that then she would never have got through a childhood like hers. From an early age she'd learnt there were more important things to worry about than whether you had holes in your shoes or your coat needed darning. She'd learnt that good health—the one thing money couldn't buy—was the only thing worth having. 'I believe it's best to be respectful of other people's feelings and that your parents might be confused and possibly upset if they realise we don't really know one another. But the main reason I need to know about you is because I'm having your baby.' She saw the increased darkening of his eyes—as if she had reminded him of something he would rather forget. But he couldn't forget it, and neither could she. 'I don't know anything about your childhood,' she finished simply. 'Nothing at all.'

He appeared to consider her words before expelling a slow breath of air. 'Very well. First and foremost you must understand that I am a Neapolitan to the very core of my being.' His voice became fierce, and proud. 'And that I have a great passion for this beautiful city of mine.'

So why don't you live here? Molly thought suddenly. *Why do you only ever visit at Christmas?* But she said nothing, just absorbed his words the way she'd absorbed other people's words all her working life.

'I grew up in the Rione Sanità, a very beautiful area, which is rich with history.' There was a pause. 'But it is also one of the poorest places in the city.'

'You?' she echoed disbelievingly, unable to hold back her shocked reaction. 'Poor?'

He smiled cynically as he flicked a disparaging finger towards his sleek suit jacket. 'You think I was born wearing fine clothes like these, Molly? Or that my belly never knew hunger?'

Yes, that was exactly what she'd thought, mainly because Salvio De Gennaro wore his wealth supremely well. He acted as if he'd never known anything other than handmade shoes and silk shirts, and people to drive his cars and planes for him. 'You've come a long way,' she said slowly. 'What happened?'

'What happened was that I had a talent,' he told her simply. 'And that talent was football. The moment my foot touched a ball, I felt as if I had found what I was born to do. I used to play every moment I could. There was nowhere suitable close to my home so I found a derelict yard to use. I marked a spot on the wall and I used to hit that same spot over and over again. Word got out and people used to come and watch me. They used to challenge me to see how long I could keep the ball in the air and sometimes I used to take their bets because many of them thought they could put a ball past me. But I could always score, even if there were two people against me in goal. And then one day the scouts turned up and overnight my whole life changed.'

'What happened?' she prompted as his words faded away.

Salvio stared out of the window, drinking in the sapphire beauty of the bay. Would it sound boastful to tell her he'd been called the greatest footballer of his generation? Or that the superstar lifestyle had arrived far more quickly than expected? 'I trained every hour that God sent, determined to fulfil all that early promise, and very quickly I was signed by one of the country's most prestigious clubs where I scored a record number of goals. I knew success, and fame, and for a while it was a crazy life. Everywhere I went, people would stop me and want to talk about the game and I don't remember the last time I was made to pay for a pizza.'

'But...something went wrong?' she observed. 'I mean, badly wrong?'

He narrowed his eyes. Was her blithe comment about knowing nothing of his past just another of the lies which slipped so easily from women's lips? 'What makes you ask that?'

She hesitated. 'I'm not sure. Maybe the note of finality in your voice. The look of...'

'Of what, Molly?' he demanded. 'And please don't just give me the polite answer you think I ought to hear.'

She met his eyes, surprised at his perception because she had been about to do exactly that. 'Bitterness, I guess,' she said. 'Or maybe disappointment.'

He wanted to deny her accusations—if that was what they were—but he couldn't. And suddenly he found himself resenting her astuteness and that gentle look of understanding which had softened her face. He'd agreed to tell her the basics—not for her to start peeling back the layers so that she could get a closer look at his damned soul. So why did he continue with his story, as if now he'd lifted the lid on it, he found it impossible to put it back?

'I'll tell you what happened,' he said roughly, becoming aware of the heavy beat of his pulse at his temple. 'My life was a fairy tale. It wasn't just the success, or the money—and the chance to do good stuff with all that money—it was the fact that I loved playing football. It was the only thing I ever wanted to do. And then one day I was brought down by an ugly tackle and tore my cruciate ligament. Badly.' His mouth twisted. 'And that was the end of the fairy tale. I never played again.'

Silence followed his stark statement and then she spoke in that soft voice. 'Oh, Salvio, that must have—'

'Please. Spare me the platitudes,' he ground out, hardening his heart to the distress which had made her eyes grow as dark as storm clouds—because he didn't need her sympathy. He didn't need anything from any-

one. He'd learnt what a mistake *that* could be. 'The injury I could have learned to live with. After all, every
professional sportsman or woman has to accept that one
day their career will end—even if that happens sooner
than they wanted. What made it worse was the discov-
ery that my manager had been systematically working his way through my fortune before leaving town.'
There was a pause. 'Suddenly, everything I thought I
had was gone. No job. No money. My fall from grace
was…spectacular.'

'So what did you do?' she whispered.

Salvio shrugged. He had raged for several days and
thought seriously about going after his manager and
pinning him to the nearest wall until he had agreed to
pay the money back. Until he'd realised that revenge
was time-consuming and ultimately damaging. That
he didn't want to spend his life in pursuit of his broken dreams and to dwell on the glories of his past, like
some sad loser. And then had come the final blow. The
final, bitter straw which had made him feel a despair he
had vowed never to repeat. Resolutely, he pushed the
memory away. 'I sold all my cars and the fancy apartment I'd bought in Rome,' he said. 'And gave most of
the proceeds to my parents. Then I took what was left
and bought a plane ticket to the US.'

'That's a long way from Naples,' she observed slowly.
'Why there?'

'Because it was a big enough place to lose myself
in and to start again. I didn't want to be defined by a
career which had been cut short and I was young and
strong and prepared to work hard.' He'd worked to the

exclusion of pretty much everything else in order to get the break he'd needed and, when it had come, he had grabbed at it with both hands. Perceptive enough to recognise that people were starting to move down-town and that run-down areas of the city were potential goldmines, he had started buying up derelict properties and then renovating them. On his Christmas trip back to Naples that first year, he had brought his mother a fancy coat from Bloomingdales. These days he could give her the entire store—and frequently tried—but no amount of material success could ever fill the empti-ness in his heart.

He stared at Molly, amazed at how much he had told her. More than he'd ever admitted to anyone, even to Lauren. His gaze raked over her and he thought how different she looked from the first time he'd seen her, eating cake in the kitchen, her ripe body looking as if it was about to burst out of her uniform. Her green dress exuded all the class and sophistication which was an inevitable by-product of wearing designer clothes which had been chosen by an expert. Yet it was the softness of her eyes he noticed most—and the dewy perfection of her creamy skin. She still radiated the same whole-some sex appeal which had drawn him to her in the first place and he wondered why he was wasting time talk-ing like this. What would he be doing with any other woman he was sharing a bedroom with—let alone the one who was wearing his ring?

He felt the erratic hammer of his pulse as he glanced down at his watch. 'I don't want to talk about the past any more.'

'Okay,' she said cautiously. 'Then we won't.'

'And we don't have to be at my folks' place for a while,' he said unevenly. 'Do you want a tour of the city?'

'Is that what you'd like to do?' she questioned, with the compliance which was such an essential part of her nature.

'No. That's the last thing I want to do right now. I can think of a much better way to pass the next couple of hours. Can't you?'

Molly thoughts were teeming as she met his dark gaze. So much of what he'd told her hadn't been what she was expecting, yet now she knew the facts they didn't really come as a surprise. The first time she'd seen him she'd noticed the power-packed body of a natural sportsman and the faint limp which he had all but managed to disguise. The single physical flaw in a man who was looking at her now with a question in his eyes.

She was still a relative novice at sex, but already she could recognise the desire which was making his face grow tense. She knew what he wanted. What *she* wanted too. Because she hadn't really enjoyed their night apart, last night. And even though the bed had been amazingly comfortable, she kept thinking about Salvio lying next door. Wondering why he hadn't tried a bit harder to sleep with her. Wondering if he'd gone off her and didn't fancy her any more. And—desire aside—wasn't the truth that she felt *safe* in his arms—even if that feeling passed as quickly as a summer storm? She stared into his molten black eyes and, for once, said exactly what was in her heart.

'Yes, I can think of a few things I'd like to do,' she agreed shyly. 'As long as they involve us being horizontal.'

She was unprepared for the curve of his smile as he walked towards her or for the way he lifted her hand to his, kissing each finger in turn before leading her over to the huge bed which overlooked the famous bay. She was eager to feel his naked skin against hers but this time there was no urgency as he began to undress her. This time his fingers were leisurely as they unclipped her bra and her swollen breasts came spilling out, his moan appreciative as he caught one taut nipple between his teeth. Molly squirmed beneath the teasing flick of his tongue but her frustration didn't seem to have any effect on his lazy pace. And didn't her heart pound with joy when he bent his head to drop a series of tender kisses on her belly as if he was silently acknowledging the tiny life which grew inside her?

'S-Salvio?' she stumbled tentatively as she felt the brush of his lips against her navel.

'It's going to be okay,' he said, his voice growing husky.

What was he talking about—their future, or meeting his parents? Or both?

But suddenly Molly was beyond caring as his movements became more urgent.

She cried out when he entered her and clung to him fiercely as he made each hard thrust. It felt so deep— he seemed to be filling her body completely, as if he couldn't get enough of her. And it felt different, more *intimate* than it had ever been before. Was that because he'd trusted her enough to tell her things she suspected he usually kept locked away—or was this sudden closeness all in her imagination? But the pleasure she was experiencing wasn't imaginary. Her senses felt exquisitely raw and heightened so that when her orgasm came, Molly felt as if rocked by a giant and powerful wave— her satisfaction only intensified by the moan he gave as he spilled his seed inside her. Afterwards she felt as if she were floating on a cloud. His breath was warm and comforting against her neck and she missed his presence when he withdrew from her and rolled to the other side of the mattress.

'That was just...perfect,' she said dreamily, the words out of her mouth before she could prevent them.

But Salvio didn't answer and, although the sound of his breathing was strong and steady, Molly wasn't sure whether or not he was asleep. Was he just lying there ignoring her? she wondered, with a sudden streak of paranoia. Lying there and *pretending*?

But she decided it was pointless to get freaked out by his sudden detachment, even if she'd had the energy to do so. Nestling herself down into the big mound of feathery pillows, Molly gave a little sigh and fell asleep.

CHAPTER NINE

Perhaps inevitably, they slept for longer than they'd intended and Molly woke with a start, looking round in mild confusion as she tried to get her bearings. Maybe they'd been catching up on too many restless nights, or maybe the amazing sex they'd just enjoyed had taken it out of them. Either way, the Neapolitan sky outside their hotel suite was ebony-dark and sprinkled with stars and when she glanced at her watch, she saw to her horror that it was almost seven—and they were due at Salvio's parents for Christmas Eve dinner in just over an hour.

'Wake up,' she urged, giving her sleeping fiancé's shoulder a rough shake. 'Or we're going to be late!'

Hurrying into the bathroom, she had the fastest shower on record before addressing the thorny issue of what to wear when meeting Salvio's parents for the first time. She still wasn't used to having quite so many clothes at her disposal and was more than a little dazzled by the choice. After much consideration, she opted for a soft knee-length skirt worn with a winter-white sweater and long black boots. Taking a deep breath, she did a little pirouette.

'Do you think your mother will approve of what I'm wearing?' she asked anxiously.

Salvio's black gaze roved over her in leisurely appraisal, before he gave a nod of approval. 'Most certainly,' he affirmed. 'You look demure and decent.'

Molly's fixed smile didn't waver as they stepped into the penthouse elevator, but really...*demure* and *decent* didn't exactly set the world on fire, did they?

They reached the lobby and as the doorman sprang forward to welcome them, Molly became aware of the buzz of interest their appearance was creating. Or rather, Salvio's appearance. She could see older men staring at him wistfully while women of all ages seemed intent on devouring him with hungry eyes. Yet despite the glamour of the female guests who were milling around the lobby, Molly felt a sudden shy pride as he took her arm and began guiding her towards the waiting car. Because *she* was the one he'd just been making love to, wasn't she? And *she* was the one who was carrying his child.

The luxury car was soon swallowed up in heavy traffic and before long they drew up outside an elegant house not too far from their hotel. Molly's nerves—which had been growing during the journey—were quickly dissolved when they were met by a tiny middle-aged woman dressed in Christmas red, her eyes dark and smiling as she opened the door to them. She hugged Molly fiercely before drawing back to look at her properly.

'At last! I have a daughter!' she exclaimed, in fluent though heavily accented English, before turning to her son and rising up on tiptoe to kiss him on each cheek, a faint note of reproof in her voice. 'And what I would like to know is why you are staying in a hotel tonight instead of here at home with your parents, Salvatore De Gennaro?'

'Because you would have insisted on us having separate rooms and this is the twenty-first century, in case you hadn't noticed,' answered her son drily. 'But don't worry, Mamma. We will be back again tomorrow.'

Slightly mollified, Rosa De Gennaro ushered them towards a beautiful high-ceilinged sitting room, where her husband was waiting and Molly stepped forward to greet him. Tall and silver-haired, Paolo De Gennaro had handsomely-rugged features which echoed those of his son and Molly got a poignant glimpse of what Salvio might look like when he was sixty. *Will I still know him when he's sixty?* she wondered, unprepared for the dark fear which shafted through her and the sudden shifting sense of uncertainty. But she shelved the useless thought and concentrated on getting to know the older couple whose joy at their son's engagement was evident. As Rosa examined her glittering ring with murmurs of delight, Molly felt a flash of guilt. What if they knew the truth? That the only reason she was here on Christmas Eve, presenting this false front of togetherness with their son, was because one reckless night had ended up with an unplanned baby.

But guilt was a futile emotion and she tried to make the best of things, the way she always did. The house seemed full of light and festivity—with the incomparable air of expectation which always defined the night before Christmas, no matter how much you tried to pretend it didn't. A beautiful tree, laden with gifts, was glittering in one of the windows and she could detect delicious smells of cooking from elsewhere in the house.

It was a long time since she'd been at the centre of a family and Molly found herself wondering what Robbie was doing tonight. She'd tried to ring him earlier that day but he hadn't picked up. *Please don't let him be gambling,* she prayed silently. *Let him have realised that there's more to life than debt and uncertainty and chasing impossible dreams.* Staring down at the nativity set which stood on a small table next to the tree, she focussed on the helpless infant in the tiny crib and tried to imagine what her own baby would look like. Would he or she resemble Salvio, with those dark stern features and a mouth which rarely smiled, but which when it did was like no other smile she'd ever seen?

She remembered the way he'd kissed her belly just before they'd made love and felt a stir of hope in her heart. He'd certainly never done *that* before—and surely that response hadn't been faked? Because the fleeting tenderness she thought she'd detected had meant just as much as the sexual excitement which had followed. And wasn't tenderness a good place to start building their relationship?

Refusing champagne and sipping from a glass of fruit juice, Molly was laughing as she examined a photo of a fourteen-year-old Salvio holding aloft a shining silver trophy, when she felt a brief pain, low in her belly. Did she flinch? Was that why Salvio's mother guided her towards a high-backed brocade chair and touched her gently on her shoulder?

'*Per piacere.* Sit down, Molly. You must be tired after your travels—but soon we will eat. You are hungry, I hope?'

Obediently, Molly took the chair she'd been offered, wondering why people were always telling her to sit down. Did she look permanently tired? Probably. Actually, she *was* a bit tired. She thought about the reason for her fatigue and her heart gave a little skip as she smiled at Salvio's mother.

'Very hungry,' she said.

'Here in Southern Italy we are proud of our culinary traditions,' Rosa continued before directing a smile at her son. 'For they represent the important times that families spend together.'

Soon they were tucking into a feast of unbelievable proportions. Molly had never *seen* a meal so big, as dish followed dish. There was spaghetti with clams and then fried shellfish, before an eel-like fish was placed in the centre of the elegant dining table with something of a flourish.

'*Capitone!*' announced Rosa. 'You know this fish, Molly? No? It is a Neapolitan tradition to eat it on Christmas Eve. In the old days, my mother used to buy it from the market while it was still alive, and then keep it in the bath until it was time to cook it. Do you remember the year it escaped, Salvio—and hid under your bed? And you were the only one brave enough to catch it?'

As his parents laughed Molly sneaked a glance at Salvio and tried to imagine the billionaire tycoon as a little boy, capturing an elusive fish which had slithered underneath a bed. Just as she tried to imagine him cradling an infant in those powerful arms, but that was too big a stretch of the imagination. At times he was so cool and distant—it was only in bed that he seemed to let his guard down and show any real feeling. She stared at the small piece of *capitone* left on her plate, wondering how it was going to work when she had his baby. She'd already established that his London penthouse wasn't particularly child-friendly—but where else would they live? He'd mentioned other houses in different countries but none of them had sounded like home, with the possible exception of his Cotswolds manor house.

They finished the meal with hard little biscuits called *rococo* and afterwards Molly insisted on helping her hostess clear the table. Efficiently, she dealt with the left-over food and dishes in a way which was second nature to her, washing the crystal glasses by hand and carefully placing them on the draining board to dry, while asking her hostess questions about life in Naples. She was just taking off the apron she'd borrowed when she noticed Rosa standing in the doorway of the kitchen watching her, a soft smile on her face.

'Thank you, Molly.'

'It was my pleasure, Signora De Gennaro. Thank you for a delicious meal. You have a wonderful home and you've been very welcoming.'

'*Prego.*' Rosa gave a small nod of satisfaction. 'I have been waiting many years for a daughter-in-law and I think you will be very good for my son.'

Molly's heart pounded as she hung the apron on a

hook beside the door, hoping Rosa didn't want to hear the romantic story of how she and her son had first met. Because there wasn't one. She suspected the truth would shock this kindly woman but Molly couldn't bear to tell her any lies. *So concentrate on the things you* can *say*, she told herself fiercely. *On all the things you wish would happen.*

'Oh, I hope I will be,' she said, her voice a little unsteady as she realised she meant every word. 'I want to be the best wife I can.'

Rosa nodded, her dark eyes intense and watchful. 'You are not like his other girlfriends,' she said slowly.

Was that a good thing or a bad thing? Molly wondered. 'Aren't I?'

'Not at all.' Rosa hesitated. 'Though he only ever brought one other to meet us.'

Molly stilled, telling herself it would be foolish to ask any more questions. But she hadn't factored in curiosity—and curiosity was a dangerous thing. Wasn't it the key which turned the lock in an invisible door—exposing you to things you might be better not knowing? And the crazy thing was even though she *knew* that, it didn't stop her from prying. 'Oh?' she questioned. Just one little word but that was all it took.

'She was no good for him,' said Rosa darkly, after a brief pause. '*Sì*, she was very beautiful but she cared only for his fame. She would never have helped with the dishes like this. She wanted to spend her Christmases in New York, or Monaco.' She touched her fingertips to the small golden cross at her neck. 'I give thanks that he never married her.'

Married her? Molly's heart constricted. Had Salvio been engaged to someone else? The man who had told her he didn't 'do' emotion? The nebulous twist of pain in her stomach which she'd felt earlier now returned with all the ferocity of a hot spear, which Molly bore behind the sunniest smile in her repertoire. But she was relieved when Salvio phoned his driver to take them back to the hotel, and leaned back weakly against the car seat, closing her eyes and willing the pain to leave her.

'Are you okay?' questioned Salvio beside her.

No, I'm not okay. I discovered tonight that you were going to marry someone else and you didn't tell me. That even though I'm carrying your baby you don't trust me enough to confide in me.

But she couldn't face a scene in the car, so she stuck to the positive. 'I'm fine!' she said brightly, still with that rictus smile in place. 'Your parents are lovely,' she added in a rush.

'Yes,' he said, and smiled. 'They liked you.'

But Molly thought he seemed lost in thought as he stared out at the festive lights of his city. Was he thinking about his other fiancée and comparing the two women? She found herself wondering why they had broken up and wondered if she would summon up the courage to ask him.

But the cramps in her stomach were getting worse. Cramps which felt horribly familiar, but which she tried to dismiss as stress. The stress of meeting his parents for the first time, or maybe the stress of discovering that she wasn't the only woman he'd asked to marry. She found herself breathing a sigh of relief when they arrived back in their penthouse suite and she unbuttoned her coat.

'Would you mind if I checked on my emails?' Salvio said as he removed the coat from her shoulders. 'I just want to see if something has come in from Los Angeles, before everything shuts down for the holidays.'

'No, of course I don't mind,' she said weakly, aware that he was already disappearing towards his computer.

She slipped into the bathroom and locked the door behind her, when she felt a warm rush between her legs and the sudden unexpected sight of blood made Molly freeze. She began to tremble.

It couldn't be.

Couldn't be.

But it was. Of course it was. On a deeper level she'd known all evening that this was about to happen, but the reality was harsher than she ever could have imagined. Her fingers clutched the cold rim of the bathtub as her vision shifted in and out of focus. She found herself wishing she were alone so that she could have given into the inexplicable tears which were welling up in her eyes. But she wasn't alone. She dashed the tears away with the tips of her fingers and tried to compose herself. Out in that fancy hotel room on the night before Christmas was her fiancé...except that the reason he'd slid these diamonds on her finger no longer existed. He would be free now, she thought—as a silent scream of protest welled up inside her.

She found her wash-bag, praying she might find what she needed—but there was no gratitude in her heart when she did, only the dull certainty of what she needed to say to Salvio. But she was loath to go out and face him. To utter the words he would probably be relieved to hear. She didn't think she could face his joy—not when she was experiencing such strange and bitter heartache.

Straightening up, she stared into the mirror, registering the pallor of her face, knowing that she couldn't tell him now. Not tonight. Not when the bells of Naples were peeling out their triumphant Christmas chorus about the impending birth of a baby.

CHAPTER TEN

'So when…?' There was a pause. 'When exactly were you going to tell me, *bedda mia*?'

The words left Salvio's lips like icy bullets but he knew immediately that his aim had been accurate. He could tell by the way Molly froze as she came out of the bathroom, the white towelling robe swathing her curvy body like a soft suit of armour.

'Tell you what?' she questioned.

Maybe if she'd come straight out and admitted it, he might have gone more easily on her but instead he felt the slow seep of anger in his veins as her guileless expression indicated nothing but a lie. A damned lie. His mouth hardened. 'That you aren't pregnant.'

She didn't deny it. She just stood in front of him, the colour leeching from her face so that her milky skin looked almost transparent. 'How did you…?' He saw the sudden flash of fear in her eyes. 'How did you know?'

Her confirmation only stoked the darkness which was building inside him. 'You think I am devoid of all my senses?' he demanded. 'That I wouldn't wonder why you turned away from me last night, then spent hours clinging to the other side of the mattress...pretending to be *asleep*?' he finished with contempt.

'So it's because we didn't have sex,' she summarised dully.

'No, not just because of that, nor even because of the way you disappeared into the bathroom when we got back from my parents' house and refused to look me in the eye,' he iced back. 'I'm not stupid, Molly. Don't you realise that a man can tell when a woman is menstruating? That she looks different. Smells different.'

'How could I ever be expected to match your encyclopaedic knowledge of women?' she questioned bitterly. 'When you're the first man I've ever slept with.'

Salvio felt the pounding of a pulse at his temple. Was she using her innocence as a shield with which to defend herself? To deflect him from a far more disturbing possibility, but one he couldn't seem to shake off no matter how hard he tried. 'Or maybe you were never even pregnant in the first place,' he accused silkily.

She reacted by swaying and sinking down onto a nearby sofa, as if his accusation had taken away her ability to stand. 'You think *that*?' she breathed, her fingers spreading out over her throat as if she was in danger of choking.

'Why shouldn't I think that?' he demanded. 'I've never actually seen any proof, have I? Is that why you didn't want to tell my parents about the baby—not because it was "too early" but because there *was* no baby?'

'You really believe—' she shook her damp hair in disbelief '—that I would lie to you about something as important as that?'

'How should I know what you'd do if you were desperate enough? We both know you were having trouble paying off your brother's debt and that marriage to me would mean the debt would be wiped out overnight.' His gaze bored into her. 'And I was careful that night, Molly. You know I was.'

She was still staring at him as if he were the devil incarnate. 'You're saying that I…made it up? That the whole pregnancy was nothing but an *invention*?'

'Why not? It's not unheard of.' He shrugged. 'It happens less often these days but I understand in the past it was quite a common device, used by women keen to get a wedding ring on their finger.' His mouth hardened. 'Usually involving a wealthy man.'

Her body tensed and Salvio saw the change in her. Saw the moment when her habitual compliance became rebellion. When outrage filled her soft features with an unfamiliar rage which she was directing solely at him. Her eyes flashing pewter sparks, she sprang to her feet, damp hair flying around her shoulders.

'I *was* pregnant,' she flared, her hands gesturing wildly through the empty air. 'One hundred per cent pregnant. I did two tests, one after the other—and if you don't believe me, then that's your problem! And yes, I was waiting until this morning to tell you, because last night I just couldn't face having the kind of discussion we're having now. So if keeping the news to myself for less than twelve hours is harbouring some dark secret, then yes—I'm guilty of that. But I'm not the only one with secrets, am I, Salvio?'

He heard the allegation in her voice as he met her

furious gaze full on and braced himself for what was coming next.

'When were you going to let me know you'd been engaged before?' she continued, her voice still shaking with rage. 'Or weren't you going to bother?'

His eyes narrowed. 'My mother told you?'

'Of course your mother told me—how else would I know?'

'What did she say?'

'Enough.' Her voice wobbled. 'I know the woman you were going to marry was rich and I'm not. I know she was beautiful and I'm not.'

Something about the weariness in her tone made Salvio feel a sharp pang of guilt. He stared at her shadowed eyes. At the milky skin now tinged with the dull flush of fury. At the still-drying shiny hair and the voluptuous curves which had lured him like a siren's call into her arms. And he felt an unexpected wave of contrition wash over him.

'You *are* beautiful,' he stressed.

'Please. Don't,' she said, holding up her hand to silence him. 'Don't make things even worse by telling me lies!'

Her dignified response surprised him. Had he been expecting gratitude for his throwaway compliment about her looks? Was he, in his own way, as guilty as Lady Avery had been of underestimating her? Of treating her like an object, rather than a person—as someone born to serve rather than to participate? Did he think he could behave exactly as he liked towards her and she would just take it?

'You *are* beautiful,' he affirmed, as repentance flowed through him. 'And yes, I was engaged before. I didn't tell you because...'

'Because it's too painful for you to remember, I suppose?'

The pulse at Salvio's temple now flickered. In a way, yes, very painful—though not in the way he suspected she meant. It was more about the betrayal he'd suffered than anything else because, like all Neapolitans, he had an instinctive loathing of treachery. It had come as a shock to realise that Lauren hadn't loved him—only what he represented. He gave a bitter smile. Perhaps he should have had a little more empathy for Molly since he too had been treated like an object in his time. 'It happened a long time ago,' he said slowly. 'And there seemed no reason to rake it up.'

She looked at him in exasperation. 'Don't you know anything about women? On second thought, don't answer that since we've already proved beyond any reasonable doubt that what you don't know about women probably isn't worth knowing. Except maybe you don't know just how far you can push them before they finally snap.' She tugged the towelling belt of her white robe a little tighter. 'Who was she, Salvio?'

Salvio scowled. Did he really have to tell her? Rake up the bitterness all over again? He expelled air from his flared nostrils, recognising from the unusually fierce expression on Molly's face that he had to tell her. 'Her name was Lauren Meyer,' he said reluctantly. 'I met her at an official function on a pre-season tour of America and brought her back here with me to Naples.'

'And she was blonde, I suppose?'

'Yes, she was blonde,' he said, ignoring her sarcastic tone. 'What else do you want to know, Molly? That she was an heiress and that she loved fame and fortune, in that order?'

'Did she?'

'She did. She met me when I had everything.' He gave a short laugh. 'And dumped me the moment I lost it all.'

'So, what…happened?' she said, into the silence which followed.

Salvio's lips tightened, because Lauren had been the catalyst. The reason he had kissed goodbye to emotion and battened up his heart. During his career there had been plenty of women who had lusted after his body and his bank account—but he'd made the mistake of thinking that Lauren was different.

His gaze flicked over to the dark sweep of the bay before returning to the grey watchfulness in Molly's eyes and suddenly he was finding it easy to talk about something he never talked about. 'After the accident, she came to visit me. Every day she sat by my bedside, always in a different outfit, looking picture-perfect. Always ready to smile and pose for the photographers who were camped outside the hospital. She was there when the physiotherapists worked on my leg and she was there when the doctor told me I'd never play professional football again. I'll never forget the look on her face.' His laugh was harsh. 'When I was discharged, she didn't come to meet me, but I thought I knew the reason why. I went home expecting a surprise party because she loved parties, and that's when I discovered she'd flown back to the States and was seeing some all-American boy her parents wanted her to marry all along. And that was that. I never saw her again.'

There was a pause while she seemed to take it all in.

'Oh, Salvio, that's awful,' she said. 'It must have felt like a kick in the teeth when you'd lost everything else.'

'I didn't tell you because I wanted your pity, Molly. I told you because you wanted to know. So now you do.'

'And, did you…did you love her?'

He felt a twist of anger. Why did women always do this? Why did they reduce everything down to those three little words and place so much store by them? He knew what she wanted him to say and that he was going to have to disappoint her. Because he couldn't rewrite the past, could he? He was damned if he was going to tell her something just because it was what he suspected she wanted to hear. And how could he possibly dismiss lies as contemptible if he started using them himself?

'Yes, I loved her,' he said, at last.

Molly hid her pain behind the kind of look she might have presented to Lady Avery if she'd just been asked to produce an extra batch of scones before teatime, and not for the first time she was grateful for all the training she'd had as a servant. Grateful for the mask-like calm she was able to project while she tried to come to terms with her new situation. Because in less than twelve hours she'd lost everything, too. Not just her baby but her hopes for the future. Hope of being a good wife and mother. Hope that a baby might help Salvio loosen up and become more human. And now it was all gone—whipped away like a rug being pulled from beneath her feet. There was no illusion left for her to cling to. No rosy dreams. Just a man who had once loved another woman and didn't love her. A man who had accused her of lying about her baby.

A baby which was now no more.

She wanted to bury her face in her hands and sob out her heartbreak but somehow she resisted the compelling urge. Instead she chose her words as carefully as a resigning politician. 'I don't want to upset your parents but obviously I can't face going for lunch today. I mean, there's no point now, is there? I don't think I'm capable of pretending everything's the same as it was—especially on Christmas Day. I think your mother might see right through me and there's no way I want to deceive her. So maybe it's best if I just disappear and leave you to say whatever you think is best.' She swallowed. 'Perhaps you could arrange for your plane to take me back to England as soon as possible?'

Salvio stared at her, unprepared for the powerful feeling which arrowed through his gut. Was it *disappointment*? Yet that seemed much too bland a description. Disappointment was what you felt if there was no snow on the slopes during a skiing holiday, or if it rained on your Mediterranean break.

He furrowed his brow. After Lauren he'd never wanted marriage. He'd never wanted a baby either but, having been presented with a *fait accompli*, had done what he considered to be the right thing by Molly. And of *course* it had affected him, because, although his heart might be unfeeling, he was discovering he wasn't made of stone. Hadn't he allowed himself the brief fantasy of imagining himself with a son? A son he could teach to kick a ball around and to perfect the *elastico* move for which he'd been so famous?

Only now Molly wanted to leave him. Her womb was empty and her spirit deflated by his cruel accusations and she was still staring at him as if he were some kind of monster. Maybe he deserved that because hadn't she only ever been kind and giving? Rare attributes which only a fool would squander—and he was that fool.

'No. Don't go,' he said suddenly.

She screwed up her eyes. 'You mean you won't let me use your plane?'

'My plane is at your disposal any time you want it,' he said impatiently. 'That's not what I mean.' His mouth hardened. 'I don't want you to go, Molly.'

'Well, I've got to go. I can't hang around pretending nothing's happened, just because you don't want to lose face with your parents.'

'It has nothing to do with losing face,' he argued. 'It has more to do with wanting to make amends for all the accusations I threw at you. About realising that maybe—somehow—we could make this work.'

'Make *what* work?'

'This relationship.'

She shook her head. 'We don't have a relationship, Salvio.'

'But we could.'

She narrowed her eyes. 'You're not making any sense.'

'Aren't I?' He lowered his voice. 'I get the feeling you weren't too unhappy about having my baby.'

She stared down at her feet and as he followed the direction of her gaze, he noticed her toenails were un-varnished. It occurred to him that he'd never been in-timate with a woman whose life hadn't been governed by beauty regimes and his eyes narrowed in sudden comprehension. Was that shallow of him? She looked up again and he could see the pride and dignity writ-ten all over her face and he felt the twist of something he didn't recognise deep inside him.

'If this is a soul-baring exercise then it seems only fair I should bear mine. And I couldn't help the way I felt about being pregnant,' she admitted. 'I knew it wasn't an ideal situation and should never have hap-pened but, no, I wasn't unhappy about having your baby, Salvio. It would have been...'

'Would have been what?' he prompted as her words tailed off.

Somebody to love, Molly wanted to say—but even in this new spirit of honesty, she knew that was a dec-laration too far. Because that sounded needy and vul-nerable and she was through with being vulnerable. She wished Salvio would stop asking her all this stuff, especially when it was so out of character. Why didn't he just let her fly back to England and let her get on with the rest of her life and begin the complicated pro-cess of getting over him, instead of directing that soft look of compassion at her which was making her feel most...peculiar? She struggled to remove some of the emotion from her words.

'It would have been a role which I would have happily taken on and done to the best of my ability,' she said. 'And I'm not going to deny that on one level I'm deeply disappointed, but I'll... I'll get over it.'

Her words faded into silence. One of those silences which seemed to last for an eternity when you just knew that everything hinged on what was said next, but Salvio's words were the very last Molly was expecting.

'Unless we try again, of course,' he said.

'What are you talking about?' she breathed.

'What if I told you that fatherhood was something which I had also grown to accept? Which I would have happily taken on, despite my initial reservations? What if I told you that I was disappointed, too? *Am* disappointed,' he amended. 'That I've realised I *do* want a child.'

'Then I suggest you do something about it,' she said, her words brittle as rock candy and she wondered if he had any idea how much it hurt to say them. Or how hard it was to stem the tide of tears which was pricking at her eyes. Tears not just for the little life which was no more, but for the man who had created that life. Because that was the crazy thing. That she was going to miss Salvio De Gennaro. How was it that in such a short while he seemed to have become as integral to her life as her own heartbeat? 'Find a woman. Get married. Start a family. That's the way it usually works.'

'That's exactly what I intend to do. Only I don't need to find a woman. Why would I, when there's one standing in front of me?'

'You don't mean that.'

'Don't tell me what I mean, Molly. I mean every word and I'm asking you to be my wife.'

Molly blinked in confusion. He was asking her to *marry* him—despite the fact she was no longer carrying his baby? She thought about the first time she'd ever seen him and how completely blown away she'd been. But this time she was no longer staring at him as if he were some demigod who had just tumbled from the stars. The scales had fallen from her eyes and now she saw him for what he was. A flawed individual— just like her. He had introduced her to amazing sex and fancy clothes. They'd made love on a giant bed overlooking the Bay of Naples and he had kissed her belly when a tiny child had been growing there. She had met his parents and they had liked her—treating her as if she were already part of the family. And somehow the culmination of all those experiences had changed her. She was no longer the same humble person who would accept whatever was thrown at her. The things which had happened had allowed her to remove the shackles which had always defined her. She no longer felt like a servant, but a woman. A real woman.

Yet even as that realisation filled her with a rush of liberation, she was at pains to understand why Salvio was making his extraordinary proposition. He was off the hook now. He was free again. Surely he should be celebrating her imminent departure from his life instead of trying to postpone it?

'Why do you want to marry me?' she demanded.

His gaze raked over her but this time it was not his usual sensual appraisal—more an impartial assessment of her worth. 'I like your softness and kindness,' he said slowly. 'Your approach to life and your work ethic. I think you will make a good mother.'

'And that's all?' she found herself asking.

He narrowed his eyes. 'Surely that is enough?'

She wasn't certain. If you wrote down all those things they would make a flattering list but the glaring omission was love. But Salvio had loved once before and his heart had been broken and damaged as a result. Could she accept his inability to love her as a condition of their marriage, and could they make it work in spite of that?

Behind him, Naples was framed like a picture-postcard as he began to walk towards her and for once his limp seemed more pronounced than usual. And although the thrust of his thighs was stark evidence enough of his powerful sensuality, it was that tiny glimpse of frailty which plucked at her heartstrings.

'I wanted this baby,' he said simply.

Her heart pounded—not wanting to be affected by that powerful declaration. But of course she *was* affected—for it was the most human she had ever seen him. 'You had a funny way of showing it.'

He lifted his shoulders as if to concede the point. 'I'm not going to deny that at first I felt trapped. Who wouldn't in that kind of situation? But once I'd got my head around it, my feelings began to change.'

Molly felt the lurch of hope. Could she believe him? Did she dare to? She remembered the way he'd kissed her belly yesterday—and how loving she'd felt towards him as a result. And that was dangerous. When she stopped to think about it, everything about this situation was dangerous. 'So this time you're not asking me to marry you because you have to?' she continued doggedly. 'You're saying you actually *want* to?'

'Yes.' His shadowed jaw tightened. 'I do. For old-fashioned reasons rather than the unrealistic expectations of romantic love. I want a family, Molly. I didn't realise how much until the possibility was taken away from me. I want someone to leave my fortune to—because otherwise what's the point of making all this money? Someone to take my name and my genes forward. Someone who will be my future.'

Molly's heart clenched as she listened to his heartfelt words. She thought of his pain when he'd lost his career and fortune in quick succession. She thought about the woman who had betrayed him at the worst possible time. The woman he had loved. No wonder he had built a wall around his heart and vowed never to let anyone touch that heart again. She drank in the hardness of his beautiful face. Could she dismantle that wall, little by little, and would he allow her close enough to try? She knew it was a gamble—and, despite all the stern lectures she'd given her little brother, a gamble she intended to take, because by now she couldn't imagine a life without him.

But if she was to be his wife then she must learn to be his equal. There had been times in the past when she'd told Salvio what she thought he wanted to hear because that was all part of her training as a servant. But it wasn't going to be like that from now on. From now on they were going to operate on a level playing field.

'Yes, I will be your wife,' she said, in a low and un-emotional voice.

He laughed, softly. 'You drive me crazy, Molly Miller,' he said. 'Do you realise that?'

The look she gave him was genuine. 'I don't know how.'

'I think,' he observed drily, 'that's the whole point. Now come here.'

He was pulling her into his arms and for a moment Molly felt uncertain, because she had her period and surely... But the touch of his fingertips against her cheek was comforting rather than seeking and the warmth of his arms consoling rather than sexual.

'I'm sorry about the baby,' he whispered against her hair, so softly that she might have imagined it.

It was the first time he had ever held her without wanting sex and Molly pressed her eyelids tightly shut, her face resting against his silky shoulder, terrified to move or to speak because she was afraid she might cry.

CHAPTER ELEVEN

THEY WERE MARRIED in Naples in a beautiful church not far from the home of Salvio's parents. The ancient building was packed with people Molly barely knew— friends of the family, she guessed, and high-powered friends of Salvio's who had flown in from all around the world. Most of them she'd met the previous evening during a lavish pre-wedding dinner, but their names had flown in one ear and out of the other, no matter how hard she'd tried to remember them. Her mind had been too full of niggling concerns to concentrate on anything very much, but her main anxiety had been about Robbie.

Because Salvio had quietly arranged for her brother to fly from Australia to Naples as a pre-wedding sur-prise and Molly's heart had contracted with joy as Rob-bie had strolled into the restaurant where everyone was eating, flashing his careless smile, which had made many of the younger women swoon.

She had jumped to her feet to hug him, touched by Salvio's unexpected thoughtfulness, as she'd run her gaze over her brother in candid assessment. From the outside Robbie looked good—better than he'd looked in a long time. He was tanned and fit, his golden curls longer than she remembered, and his clothes were surprisingly well chosen. But she'd seen his faintly avaricious expression as he'd taken in the giant ring on her finger and the expensive venue of the sea-view wedding reception.

'Well, what do you know? You did good, sis. Real good,' he'd said slowly, a gleam entering his grey eyes. 'Salvio De Gennaro is *minted*.'

She'd found herself wanting to protest that she wasn't marrying Salvio for his money but Robbie probably wouldn't have believed her, since his teenage years had been dedicated to the pursuit of instant wealth. She'd wondered if his reluctance to maintain eye contact meant that his gambling addiction had returned. And had then wondered if she was simply transferring her own fears onto her brother.

But she wasn't going to be afraid because she was walking into this with her eyes open. She'd made the decision to be Salvio's wife because deep down she wanted to, and she was going to give the marriage everything she could. Who said that such a strangely conceived union couldn't work? She was used to fighting against the odds, wasn't she?

Holding herself tall, she had walked slowly down the aisle wearing the dress which had been created especially for her by one of London's top wedding-dress designers. The whole couture process had been a bit of an ordeal, mainly because a pale, shiny fabric wasn't terribly forgiving when you were overendowed with curves, but Molly had known Salvio wanted her to look like a traditional bride. And in her heart she had wanted that, too.

'Your breasts are very...generous.' The dressmaker had grunted. 'We're going to have to use a minimising bra, I think.'

Molly had opened her mouth to agree until she'd remembered what she'd vowed on the day of Salvio's proposal. That she was going to be true to herself and behave like his equal because the strain of doing otherwise would quickly wear her down. And if she tried to be someone she wasn't, then surely this whole crazy set-up would be doomed.

'I think Salvio likes my breasts the way they are,' she'd offered shyly and the dressmaker had taken the pins out of her mouth, and smiled.

The look on his face when she reached the altar seemed to endorse Molly's theory—and when they left the church as man and wife, the strangest thing happened. Outside, a sea of people wearing pale blue and white ribbons were cheering and clapping and Molly looked up at Salvio in confusion as their joyful shouts filled the air.

'Some of the supporters of my old football club,' he explained, looking slightly taken aback himself. 'Come to wish me *in bocca al lupo.*'

'Good luck?' she hazarded, blinking as a battery of mobile-phone cameras flashed in her face.

'*Esattamente.* Your Italian lessons are clearly paying dividends,' he murmured into her ear, his mouth brushing against one pearl-indented lobe.

Just that brief touch was enough to make her breasts

spring into delicious life beneath the delicate material of her wedding dress and Salvio's perceptive smile made Molly blush. Lifting up her bouquet of roses to disguise the evidence of physical desire, she thought how perfectly attuned he was to her body and its needs. Their sexual compatibility had been there from the start— now all she needed to concentrate on was getting pregnant.

After the wedding they flew to their honeymoon destination of Barbados, where they were shown to a large, private villa in the vast grounds of a luxury hotel. It was the closest thing to paradise that Molly could imagine and as soon as they arrived, Salvio went for a swim while she insisted on unpacking her clothes—because she didn't quite trust anyone else to do it so neatly. *Old habits die hard*, she thought ruefully.

Knotting a sarong around her waist, she went outside where her brand-new husband was lying on a sun lounger the size of a double bed, wearing a battered straw hat angled over his eyes and nothing else. A lump rose in her throat as she watched him lying in the bright sunshine—completely at ease with his bare body which was gleaming with droplets of water drying in the sun. For a moment she couldn't actually believe she was here, with him. His wife. She swallowed. Even her title took some getting used to. Signora Molly De Gennaro.

He turned to look at her, his gaze lazy as it ran a slow and comprehensive journey from her head to the tips of her toes.

'How are you feeling?' he questioned solicitously.

Trying not to be distracted by the very obvious stirring at his groin, she nodded. 'Fine, thank you,' she said politely. 'That sleep I had on the plane was wonderful.'

'Then stop standing there looking so uncertain.' Pushing aside a tumble of cushions, he patted the space beside him on the giant sunbed. 'Come over here.'

It occurred to Molly that if she wasn't careful she would end up taking orders from him just like before, but it was probably going to take a little time to ac-climatise herself to this new life. To feel as if she had the right to enjoy these lavish surroundings, instead of constantly looking around feeling as if she ought to be cleaning them.

Aware of the sensual glitter of his eyes, she walked across the patio and sank down next to him. Straight ahead glimmered a sea of transparent turquoise, edged with sand so fine it looked like caster sugar. To her left was their own private swimming pool and any time they wanted anything—*anything at all*, as they had been as-sured on their arrival—all they had to do was to ring one of the bells which were littered around the place and some obliging servant would appear.

She stuck out her feet in front of her, still getting used to toenails which were glinting a fetching shade of coral in the bright sunshine.

'You've had a pedicure,' Salvio observed.

She blinked and looked up. 'Fancy you noticing something like that.'

'You'd be amazed what I notice about you, Molly,' he murmured. 'Is that the first one you've ever had?'

'I'm afraid it is.' She lifted her chin a little defen-sively. 'I suppose that shocks you?'

'Not really, no. And anyway—' he smiled '—I like being shocked by you.'

His hand was now on her leg and she felt his finger-tips travelling slowly over her thigh. Little by little they inched upwards and her mouth grew increasingly dry as they approached the skimpy triangle of her bikini bottoms. She swallowed as his hand came to a tanta-lising halt just before they reached the red and white gingham. 'Salvio,' she breathed.

'*Sì*, Molly?' he murmured.

'We're outside. Anyone can see us.'

'But the whole point of having a *private* villa,' he emphasised, 'is that we *can't* be seen. Haven't you ever wondered what it might be like to make love in the open air?'

She hesitated. 'Maybe,' she said cautiously.

'So why don't we do it?'

'What, now?'

'Right now.'

She swallowed. 'If you're *sure* we really can't be seen.'

'I may be adventurous,' he drawled, 'but I draw the line at rampant voyeurism.'

'Go on, then,' she whispered encouragingly.

Salvio smiled as he trailed his lips down over Mol-ly's generous cleavage which smelt faintly of coconut oil and was already warm from the sun. Through her bikini top a pert nipple sprang into life against his lips and he thought how utterly entrancing she could be with that potent combination of shyness and eagerness, de-spite her lack of experience. 'You are for my eyes only,' he added gravely, hearing her sharp intake of breath as he began to undo the sarong which was knotted around her hips. 'Except you are wearing far too much for me to be able to see you properly.'

The sarong discarded, his finger crept beneath her bikini bottoms to find her most treasured spot, where she was slick and wet. Always wet, he thought achingly. Her enjoyment of sex was so delightfully fervent that it made him instantly hard. He expelled a shuddering breath of air as she responded to his caress by reaching down to touch him intimately, and he moaned his soft pleasure. He liked the way she encircled him within those dextrous fingers and the way she slid them up and down to lightly stroke the pulsing and erect flesh. He liked the way she teased him as he had taught her to tease him and to make him wait, until he felt like her captive slave. But today his hunger would not be tempered and he could not wait, his desire for her off the scale. He had let her sleep on the plane because she had looked exhausted after the wedding, but now his appetite knew no bounds. The bikini was discarded to join the sarong as he wriggled his fingers between her legs. She jerked distractedly as he found her tight bud, her nails digging into his bare shoulders as he increased his rhythmical stroke.

'You like that,' he observed, with a satisfied purr.

'Don't...don't stop, will you?' she gasped.

He gave a low laugh. 'I have no intention of stopping, *bedda mia*. I couldn't stop, even if I wanted to.' But suddenly he no longer wanted to pleasure her with his finger and, positioning himself over her, he parted her thighs and drove into her. He groaned as she matched each urgent thrust with the accommodating jerk of her hips. He revelled in the feel of her, the taste of her and the smell of her. Was it because there was no need for a condom that sex with Molly felt even more incredible than it had done before? Or because he was the one who had taught her everything? She'd never taken a man into her mouth before him, nor sucked him until he was empty and gasping. Just as she'd never had anyone's head between her thighs other than his. He closed his eyes as excitement built at a speed which almost outpaced him. Was he really so primitive that he got some kind of thrill from having bareback sex with his one-time virgin? He drove into her again. Maybe he was.

She began to come, her moans of pleasure spiralling up from the back of her throat and hovering on the edge of a scream, so that he clamped his mouth over hers in an urgent kiss. He felt the rush of her breath in his mouth and the helpless judder of her body clenching around him—and his own response was like a powerful wave which crashed over him and pulled him under. With a groan, he ejaculated, one hand splayed underneath her bottom while the other tangled in her silken hair. Beneath the Barbadian sun he felt the exquisite pulsing of his body as passion seeped away.

For a while he just lay on top of her, dazed and contented, his head cushioned on her shoulder as he dipped in and out of sleep. But eventually he stirred, his fingertips tilting her jaw, enjoying the beatific smile which curved her lips as she opened her eyes to look at him.

'So. We have a choice,' he said slowly. 'We can get

dressed again and ring for drinks, or I can go inside and fix us something and you can stay exactly as you are, which would be my preference.'

She hesitated for a moment. 'I wouldn't mind you waiting on me for a change,' she said. 'Unless you're going to do that helpless man thing of making a mess of it because it's *domestic*, so that you'll never have to do it again.'

His mouth twitched into a smile as he rose from the lounger. 'Is that what men do?'

'In my experience—well, only my working experience, of course. Every time.'

'Not this one.' He picked up the battered straw hat which had fallen off, jamming it down so that the shadow of the brim darkened his face. 'I don't like to fail at anything, Molly.'

She watched him go. Was it that which had hurt the hardest when his life had imploded around him—the fact that he would be perceived as a failure? Had that been at the root of his reluctance to return to Naples very often? Yet he had picked himself up and started all over again. He had made a success of his life in every way, except for one. Just before they'd boarded his private jet to fly here, he'd told her how delighted his parents were that he had chosen her as his bride and she found herself thinking how skewed life could be sometimes. His mother hadn't liked Lauren Meyer, but Salvio had loved her. He'd told her that himself. And if this marriage was to continue, she must resign herself to the fact that she would only ever be second-best.

But that had been her life, hadn't it? It wasn't as

if she wasn't used to it. When you worked in other people's houses you had to put yourself second, because you were only there to help their lives function smoothly. You had to be both efficient yet invisible, because people didn't really see *you*—only the service you provided.

Did Salvio see *her*? she wondered. Or was she simply a vessel to bear his child? The woman he had transformed with his vast fortune, so that she could lie in a Barbadian paradise, looking out over an azure sea as if she'd been born to this life?

The chink of ice made her glance towards the entrance to their villa, where Salvio was standing holding two tall, frosted glasses. As he began to walk towards her she wondered how a man could look so utterly at ease, completely naked save for his sunhat.

Handing her a glass, he joined her on the lounger and for a while they sipped their drinks in silence.

'Salvio,' she said eventually, watching the ice melt in the fruity cocktail.

He turned his face towards her. 'Mmm…?'

'What am I actually going to *do*? I mean, once we get back to England and you go back to work.'

He swirled the ice around in his glass, his fingers dark against the sunlit condensation. 'Weren't we planning to have a baby?'

'Yes, we were. Are,' she corrected. 'But that might not happen straight away, might it? And I can't just sit around all the time just…*waiting*.'

There was a pause. 'You want me to find you something to do?' He studied her carefully. 'There's a charitable arm belonging to my company. Do you think you'd like to get involved in that?'

She hesitated, genuine surprise tearing through her at the realisation he must think her good enough to be a part of his organisation. But it wasn't his validation which pleased her as much as the thought that this would make her a more integral part of his life—and wasn't that what marriage was all about? 'I'd like that very much.' She smiled, but his next words killed her pleasure stone dead.

'You know your brother tapped me for a loan at the wedding?'

The glass she was holding almost slipped from her suddenly nerveless fingers and quickly Molly put it down, her cheeks flaming. *'What?'*

'He said he had an idea for a new business venture and asked if I'd like to invest in it.'

'You didn't say yes?'

'You think I'm in the habit of throwing money away? I asked him how much he had already raised, and how—but he seemed reluctant to answer.' Beneath the shadowed brim of his hat, she saw that his eyes were now as hard and as cold as jet. 'Did you know about this, Molly?'

It hurt that he should ask but, when she thought about it afterwards, why *wouldn't* he ask? Salvio had been a target for women during his playing days and had fallen for someone who saw him as nothing but a trophy husband. He made no secret of not trusting women—so why should he feel any differently about her?

'Of course I didn't know he was going to ask you,'

she said in a low voice. 'And if he'd sought my opinion I would have told him not to even think about it.'

He nodded as he stared out at the bright blue horizon and the subject was closed. But Molly's determination not to let his silky accusation ruin the rest of the day only went so far, and suddenly she was aware of the aching disappointment which made the sunny day feel as if it had been darkened by a cloud.

CHAPTER TWELVE

'So how long will you be away?' Amid the croissant-crumbed debris of their early-morning breakfast, Molly glanced across the glass dining table at Salvio, who was reading one of the Italian newspapers he had couriered to his London apartment each morning.

'Only a few days,' he said, lifting his dark head to look at her. 'I'm just flying into Los Angeles for back-to-back meetings and then out again.'

'It seems an awfully long way to go,' she observed, taking a final sip of the inky black coffee she'd learned to love and which she now drank in preference to cappuccino. 'For such a short visit.'

'It is. So why don't you come with me?' His eyes gleamed as he put the newspaper down. 'We could add on a few extra days and take the highway to San Francisco. Turn it into a holiday. You've never been to the US, have you?'

She'd never actually been further than the Isle of Wight and that had been years ago. Highly tempted, Molly considered the idea, until she remembered her own responsibilities. 'I can't. I have a lunch with the charity later.'

'You could always cancel it.'

'I can't just *cancel* it, Salvio, or it won't look like I'm committed. Like I'm only playing at being on the board just because I'm your wife.'

A smile played around the edges of his lips as he got up and moved towards her, his dark eyes glittering with an expression she knew so well. 'Which means you'll just have to be patient and wait for me to get back, *mia sposa*, even though it means you'll be without me for four whole nights. In fact, just thinking about it makes me want to kiss you.'

A kiss quickly turned into Molly being carried into their bedroom with a demonstration of that effortless mastery which still dazzled her, no matter how many times it happened. She loved the way he impatiently removed the clothes he'd only just put on and the way he explored her body as if he had just stumbled across a newly discovered treasure. She loved the warm skin-to-skin contact with this man as they tumbled hungrily onto the bed. She loved him, she suddenly realised, as he plunged deep inside her. She just couldn't help herself.

She was still feeling faintly dizzy with pleasure when Salvio returned from the shower wearing the lazy smile of the satisfied predator, and she watched him as he began to dress. 'You are insatiable,' she observed.

'And don't you just hate it?' he mocked, picking up his tie and walking over to the mirror to knot it.

She hardly ever noticed his almost imperceptible limp but she noticed it today—and something about the contrast of frailty and strength which existed in his powerful body stirred a memory in her which she had unwittingly stored away.

'Salvio?'

He stared at her reflected image in the glass. 'Mmm...?'

She hesitated. 'You remember our wedding day?'

'I'm hardly likely to forget it, am I?' he questioned drily. 'And even if I had, it wouldn't be a diplomatic thing to admit after a mere three months of marriage. What about it?'

'Well.' His response didn't sound very promising but Molly forced herself to continue. 'I was wondering whether your charitable organisation ought to include some kind of football sponsorship, which I notice it doesn't do at the moment.'

'Some kind of football sponsorship?' he repeated slowly.

'Yes. You know—you could offer a financial scheme for a promising young player from a poor background.' Again, she hesitated. 'To help the type of boy you once were,' she finished, on a rush.

There was a pause while he finished knotting his tie and when he spoke, his voice was cool. 'But I don't have anything to do with football any more, Molly. You know that. I walked away from that life many years ago.'

'Yes, I know you did. But things have moved on now. You saw all those people wearing your old club's colours who came to wish you luck on your wedding day. They...they love you, Salvio. You're a legend to them and I just thought it would be...nice...' Her words faded away. 'To give something back.'

'Oh, did you?' Moving away from the mirror, Salvio

swept his gaze over his wife, who looked all pink-cheeked and tousled as she lay amid the rumpled mess they'd just made of the bed. A muscle began to work in his cheek. He'd thought that, given her previous occupation, she would have been a rather more compliant partner than she was turning out to be. He'd thought it a generous gesture to give her a seat on the board of his charity and had expected her to be grateful to him for that. But he'd imagined her turning up regularly at meetings and sitting there quietly—not to suddenly start dishing out advice. Surely she, more than anyone, must have realised it was inappropriate as well as unwanted? 'I really don't think it's your place to start advising me on how I spend my money, Molly,' he drawled.

She went very still. 'Not *my place*?' she echoed, the colour leeching from her face and her dark lashes blinking in disbelief. 'Why not? Do you think the one-time servant should remain mute and just go along with what she's been told, rather than ever showing any initiative of her own? Are you making out like there's still all those inequalities between us, despite the fact that I now wear your ring?'

'There's no need to overreact,' he said coolly, even though that was exactly what he *did* think. 'And I really don't want an argument when I'm just about to fly to the States. We'll talk about it when I get back.' He dipped his head towards her with a smile she always found irresistible. 'Now kiss me.'

Knowing it would be childish to turn her face away, Molly attempted a close approximation of a fond kiss, but inside she was seething as the door of the apartment slammed shut behind her departing husband. She felt as if the pink cloud she'd been floating on since the day they'd wed had suddenly turned black. Was it because, behind all the outward appearances of a relatively blissful new marriage, nothing much had changed? Despite him giving her a seat on the board of his charity, it seemed she wasn't allowed to have any ideas of her own. She might be wearing his shiny gold wedding band but at that precise moment she felt exactly like the servant she'd always been. And there was another pressure, too. One she hadn't dared to acknowledge—not even to herself, let alone to Salvio.

Gloomily, she got out of bed and went to stare out of the window, where there was no sign of new life. They were already into April but spring seemed to have been put on hold by the harsh weather. Even the daffodils in the planters on Salvio's roof terrace had been squashed by the unseasonable dump of snow which had ground the city to a halt for the last few days.

No sign of life in her either.

Her hands floating down to her belly, she prayed that this month she might get the news she was longing for, even though the low ache inside her hinted at an alternative scenario. She linked her manicured fingers together, dreading another month of unspoken disappointment. Of cheerfully convincing herself it would happen eventually. Of wondering how long she could continue walking this precarious tightrope of a marriage which had only taken place because her wealthy husband wanted an heir. Because what if she *couldn't* conceive? She'd been pregnant once, yes, but there was no guarantee it would happen again. Life didn't provide guarantees like that, did it?

Forcing herself to get on with the day, she showered and dressed—slithering into a dress she wouldn't have dared to wear a few months ago, even if she could have afforded to. But her body shape had changed since living with Salvio—and not just because she'd checked out the basement gym in this luxury apartment block and discovered she liked it. She ate proper regular meals now because her Neapolitan husband's love of good food meant that he wasn't a great fan of snacks, and as a consequence she was in the best shape of her adult life.

She took a cab to her charity lunch, which was being held in the ballroom of one of the capital's smartest hotels and was today awarding acts of bravery involving animals as well as humans. She particularly enjoyed hearing about the kitten who had been rescued from the top of a chimney pot by a nineteen-year-old university drop-out who had previously been terrified of heights. She chatted to him afterwards and he told her that he'd decided he was going to train as a vet, and Molly felt a warm glow of pleasure as she listened to his story.

She was just chopping vegetables for a stir-fry when Salvio rang from Los Angeles, telling her he missed her and, although she wanted to believe him, she found herself wondering if he was just reading from a script. It was easy to say those sorts of things when he was thousands of miles away, when the reality was that he'd made her feel she'd stepped out of line this morning just because she'd dared express an opinion of her own.

Well, maybe it was time to stop drifting around in a

half-world of pretence and longing. She would sit him down when he returned from his trip and they would talk honestly because, even though the truth could hurt, it was better to know where you stood. And even though her stupid heart was screaming out its objections she couldn't keep putting it off. She would ask him if he really wanted to continue with the marriage and maybe it was better to confront that now, before there *was* a baby.

But then something happened. Something which changed everything.

It started with an email from her brother which arrived on the day Salvio was due to return from America. Robbie was notoriously unreliable at keeping in touch and she hadn't heard from him since the wedding, even though she'd sent several lovely photos of him dancing with one of Salvio's distant cousins at the reception. She hadn't even mentioned the loan he'd asked her husband for—deciding it was an issue best settled between him and Salvio.

So her smile was one of pleasure when she saw new mail from Robbie Miller, which had pinged into her inbox overnight, with the subject line: Have you seen this?

'This' turned out to be an attachment of an article taken from a newspaper website. An American newspaper, as it happened. And there, in sharp Technicolor detail, was a photograph of her husband, sitting outside some flower-decked restaurant with a beautiful blonde, the sapphire glitter of a sunlit sea in the background.

Her fingers clawed at the mouse as she scrolled down the page but somehow Molly knew who Salvio's companion was before she'd read a single word. Was it the woman's poise which forewarned her, or simply the way she leaned towards Salvio's handsome profile with the kind of intimacy which was hard-won? Her heart clenched with pain as she scanned the accompanying prose.

> *Heartthrob property tycoon Salvio De Gennaro was pictured enjoying the sea air in Malibu today.*
>
> *Newly wed to former maid Molly Miller, in a lavish ceremony which took place in the groom's native Naples, the Italian billionaire still found time to catch up with ex-fiancée Lauren Meyer.*
>
> *With the ink barely dry on her divorce papers, perhaps heiress Lauren was advising Salvio on some of the pitfalls of marriage.*
>
> *Either that, or the Californian wine was just too good to resist...*

Hands shaking, Molly stared at the screen, closing her eyes in a futile bid to quell the crippling spear of jealousy which lanced through her like a hot blade, but it was still there when she opened them again, her gaze caught by the glitter of the diamonds at her finger. The diamonds she had once compared to tears, rather than rain. But there were real tears now. Big ones which were splashing onto her trembling fingers. Pushing her chair away from the desk, her vision was blurred as blindly she stumbled into the bedroom. She rubbed her fists into her eyes but the stupid tears just kept on flowing, even though deep down she knew she had no right to feel sorrow. Because it wasn't as if theirs was a *real* relationship, was it? She had no right to be jealous of a husband who had never loved her, did she? Not really. It had only ever been a marriage of convenience—providing each of them with what they wanted.

Or rather, what she'd *thought* she'd wanted... Security and passion with a man she'd begun to care for and, ultimately, a family of her own. Only now the truth hit her with a savage blow as she forced herself to acknowledge what it was she *really* wanted. Not the fancy penthouse or the different homes dotted all around the globe. Not the platinum credit card with its obscene spending limit.

She wanted Salvio's love, she realised—and that was just a wish too far. He didn't do love—at least, not with her. But he *had* loved Lauren. And try as she might, she just couldn't put a positive spin on his reunion with his ex-fiancée in that sunny and glamorous Malibu setting. For the first time in her life she was right out of optimistic options.

There were no tears left to cry as she walked across the bedroom, but she was filled with a strange new sense of calm as she opened up the wardrobe and took out her battered old suitcase, knowing what she intended to do.

She would do the brave thing.

The right thing.

The only thing.

'Molly?' Salvio frowned as he walked into an apartment which instinct told him was empty. Yet he'd texted her to tell her he was on his way home and he'd assumed she would be waiting with that soft smile which always greeted him when he arrived home from work. 'Molly?' he called again, even though the word echoed redundantly through the quiet apartment.

He found the note quickly, as he had obviously been intended to. One of those brief notes which managed to say so little and yet so much, in just a few stark words. And sitting on top of it was her diamond ring.

Salvio.

I've seen the newspaper article about you and Lauren and I want to do the best thing, so I'm staying in a hotel until I can get a job sorted out.

I'll send you my address when I have one, so you can instruct your lawyers.

*It's been an amazing experience, so thank you for everything. And...*in bocca al lupo.

Crushing the note in an angry fist, he strode over to the computer and saw the article immediately, reading it with a growing sense of disbelief before cursing long and loud into the empty air. Why hadn't any of his staff alerted him to this? Because his assistant had been instructed to treat gossip columns with the contempt they deserved, by ignoring them. He stared at the photo, thinking that whoever said the camera didn't lie must have been delusional. Because it did. Big-time.

He saw Lauren's finely etched profile and the angled bones of her shoulder blades. Her long blonde hair was waving gently in the breeze and she was leaning forward with an earnest expression on her face. It must have been taken just before his response had made her delicate features crumple and her blue eyes darken with disbelief.

Pulling the phone from his pocket, he found Molly's number and hit the call button, unsurprised when it went straight to voicemail over and over again, and his mouth hardened. Did she think she could just walk out on him, leaving nothing but that banal little note?

Scrolling down, he found another number he used only very infrequently. His voice lowered as he began to speak in rapid Neapolitan dialect, biting out a series of terse demands before finally cutting the connection.

CHAPTER THIRTEEN

MOLLY STARED AT the richly embossed walls of the fancy hotel and the dark red lilies which were massed in a silver vase. She'd chosen the five-star Vinoly because she'd heard Salvio mention it, but as from tomorrow she would start searching for somewhere cheaper to stay. No way was she going to try to cling to the high-life she'd enjoyed during her brief tenure as his wife, because that life was over and she needed to get used to it.

The phone rang but she didn't need to look down to see who was calling. Salvio. Again. After yet another brief internal tussle she chose to ignore it, just like she'd avoided reading the texts he'd been sending. Because what was the point in hearing anything he had to say? What if his smooth weasel words tempted her back into his arms and the guarantee of heartbreak? She didn't want to hear excuses or half-truths. She wanted to preserve her sanity, even if her heart had to break in the process.

But first she needed to start looking for a job. A live-in job she could practically do with her eyes closed. She would sign up with an agency in the morning and tell them she wanted a fresh start. Somewhere she'd never been before—like Scotland, or Wales. Somewhere new so she could be completely anonymous while licking her wounds and trying to forget that for one brief shining moment she'd been the wife of a man who...

She bit her lip.

A man she'd fallen in love with, despite all her best efforts to remain immune to him.

But Salvio hadn't wanted her love. Only Lauren's. She swallowed. Was the beautiful heiress willing to give Salvio a second chance? Was that the reason behind their secret liaison when they'd been making eyes at one another in the Californian sunshine?

She didn't feel hungry but she hadn't eaten anything since breakfast and she always used to tell Robbie that your brain couldn't function properly unless you kept it nourished. Ordering a cheese omelette from room service, she thought about her brother. She hadn't replied to his email, mainly because she couldn't think of anything to say. Not yet, anyway. She wondered if he'd acted out of the goodness of his heart. If sending the proof of Salvio's clandestine meeting was a brotherly intervention to protect her from potential hurt. Or had Robbie been motivated by spite—because his wealthy new brother-in-law had refused to give him the loan he'd wanted?

She paced the room, unable to settle. Unable to shift the dark features of her husband from her mind and wondering whether she would ever be able to forget this interlude. Or to—

Her thoughts were interrupted by a loud rap on the door.

'Who is it?' Molly called out sharply.

'Room service!'

She opened the door to the woman's voice, her heart crashing against her ribcage when she saw Salvio standing there, holding a tray dominated by a silver dome. In the distance was the retreating view of a hotel employee, who'd obviously been rewarded for allowing this bizarre role-reversal to take place. Which was exactly what it felt like. Salvio in a subservient role holding a tray, and her opening the door of some swanky hotel room. Except he didn't stay subservient for very long.

'Step aside, Molly,' he clipped out.

'You can't come in.'

'Just try stopping me.'

She didn't dare. She'd never seen him look so determined as he stormed into her room. There was a clatter as he slammed the tray down and Molly shuddered to think what damage he must have inflicted on her cheese omelette. Not that she wanted it any more. How could she possibly have eaten anything when she could barely breathe?

He turned round and she was taken aback by the fury which was darkening his imposing features into an unrecognisable mask. 'Well, Molly?' he snarled.

'Well, what?' she retorted. 'How did you find me?'

'You booked this room with our joint credit card.'

'And?'

'And therefore you were traceable. I had one of my contacts look into it for me.'

She screwed up her brow. 'Isn't that...illegal?'

He shrugged. 'When a man wishes to find his errant wife then surely he will use whatever means are available to him.'

'Well, you've wasted your time because there's nothing to say!'

'I disagree. There's plenty to say, and we're having this out right now.'

And suddenly Molly knew she couldn't let him take over and dominate this situation by the sheer force of his indomitable character. Yes, he was powerful, rich and successful, but she was his wife. His *equal*, despite the inequality of their assets. That was what she'd vowed to be when she had agreed to marry him, but somewhere along the way her resolve had slipped. Was that because the more she'd started to care for him, the harder she had found it to assert herself?

Well, not any more. She needed to make it plain that, although she might not have anything of material value, she valued *herself*. And she would not allow Salvio De Gennaro to make a fool of her, or for her heart to be slowly broken by a man who was incapable of emotion.

'I saw the article from the American newspaper.'

'I know you did. Your brother sent it to you.'

'Did you find *that* out illegally, too?' she scorned.

'No, Molly. You left your computer open.'

'Well, if you'd looked a little harder you'd have seen that I also did a room search for the Vinoly hotel,' she said triumphantly. 'Which wouldn't have involved getting someone to snoop on me!'

Unexpectedly, he sighed and a sudden weariness

touched the corners of his dark eyes as he looked at her. 'What do you think I did in Los Angeles, Molly?' he questioned tiredly. 'Do you think I had sex with Lauren?'

A spear of pain shot through her. 'Did you?'

He winced as he raked his fingers back through his jet-dark hair. 'No, I did not. She heard I was in town and got in touch with me and I agreed to meet her for lunch.'

'Why?'

'Why?' He gave an odd smile. 'I thought it made sense to put away the past for good.'

'Only I suppose she'd suddenly realised the stupid mistake she'd made in letting you go?' accused Molly sarcastically.

He shrugged. 'Something like that. She is recently divorced. She asked for another chance.'

'And you said?'

There was silence for a moment and Molly actually thought that her heartbeat had grown audible—until she realised that the silver clock was thumping out the hour.

'I said I was in love with my wife,' he said simply. 'Only I'd been too stupid to show her how much.'

She shook her head, not believing him. Not believing he would ever admit to love *or* stupidity. 'I don't believe you,' she whispered.

'I know you don't and maybe I deserve that.' He hesitated, like someone who was learning the words of a new language. 'I know that at times I've been cold and difficult.'

'It isn't that, Salvio! It's the fact that you're completely backtracking on everything you said. You told me you didn't *do* love. Not any more. Remember? That you'd loved Lauren and after you broke up, you'd closed off your heart. And if that *was* true—if you really *did* love her like you claim—then how come it has all just died? Is love only a temporary thing, Salvio—which changes like the moon?'

Deeply admiring of her logic at such an intense moment, Salvio took a deep breath. He felt as if he were on a platform in front of a thousand people, about to make the most important speech of his life. And he was. But not to a thousand people. To one. To Molly. The only one who really mattered.

And his whole future hinged on it.

'I thought I loved Lauren because that's how I felt at the time,' he said, in a low voice. 'And surely it is a kind of treachery to deny the feelings we once had? That would be like trying to rewrite history.' There was a pause. 'But I see now it wasn't real love—it was a complex mixture of other stuff which I was too immature to understand.'

'What kind of stuff?' she questioned, as his voice tailed off.

'It was more to do with a young man who wanted to conquer the elusive,' he admitted. 'A man who for a while became someone he wasn't. Someone blinded by an ideal, rather than a real person—and Lauren *was* that ideal. And then I met you, Molly. The most real person in the world. You charmed me. Disarmed me. You crept beneath my defences before I even realised what was happening. You made me feel good—you still do—and not just in the obvious way. It's like I'm the best version of myself whenever you're around. Like I can achieve anything—even if my instinct is to fight against it every inch of the way, because there's a part of me which doesn't really believe that I deserve to be this happy.'

'Salvio—'

'No. Please. Let me finish,' he said and his voice was shaking now. 'You need to understand that all this is true, because there is no way I would say it if it wasn't.' His black eyes raked over her. '*Do* you believe me, Molly? That I would walk to the ends of the earth for you and further, if that's what you wanted? And that I love you in a way I've never loved before?'

Molly stared into the molten darkness of his eyes, but she didn't have to give it a lot of thought, because she did believe him. She could read it in the tender curve of his lips, even if he hadn't uttered those quietly fervent words which had rung so true. But if they were shining a spotlight on their relationship then they couldn't allow any more shadows to lurk in unexplored corners, and she needed the courage to confront what was still troubling her.

'But what about the baby?' she whispered.

'What baby?' he said gently. 'Are you trying to tell me you're pregnant?'

'I don't know. I don't think so. But that's the whole point. What if…?' She swallowed. 'What if, for some reason, I can't give you the child you long for?'

'Then we will go to the best doctors to find out why, or we will adopt. It's not a deal-breaker, Molly. Not even a deal-maker. Not any more. I want you. *You.* That's all.'

That's all? Molly blinked as for the first time she re-alised that Salvio De Gennaro was truly captivated by her. Her! A flush of pleasure heated her skin and maybe someone else in her position might have briefly revelled in her newly discovered power. But this wasn't about power. It was about love and equality. About consider-ation and respect. About loyalty and truth.

It was about them.

She smiled, the happiness swelling up in her heart making it feel as if it were about to burst open. 'I be-lieve you,' she said softly. 'And I love you. So much. I think I've always loved you, Salvio De Gennaro, and I know I always will.'

'Then you'd better come here and kiss me,' he said, in a voice which sounded pretty close to breaking. 'And convince me that this is for real.'

EPILOGUE

Salvio stared at the lights as he lay back contentedly. Rainbow-coloured lights which jostled for space among all the glittering baubles which hung from the Christmas tree. Behind the tree glittered the Bay of Naples and, inside the main reception room of their newly purchased home, he lay naked next to his beautiful Molly on a vast velvet sofa which had been chosen for precisely this kind of activity.

'Happy?' he murmured, one hand idly teasing her bare nipple while his lips lazily caressed the soft silk of her hair.

'Happy?' She nuzzled into his neck. 'So happy I can't even put it into words.'

'Well, try.'

Molly traced her finger over the loud rhythm of her husband's heart. Next door their ten-month-old son Marco lay sleeping—getting as much rest as possible in preparation for the excitement of his first Christmas. And this year, everyone was coming to *them*. Salvio's parents would be arriving later for the traditional Eve of Christmas feast. And so would Robbie, who was currently meeting the parents of Salvio's cousin, who he had recently started dating. Molly prayed he wouldn't let anyone down—most of all himself—but she was hopeful that her brother had finally sorted himself out. Much of it was down to Salvio and the well-intentioned but stern advice he had delivered. He'd told Robbie he would support him through college, but only if he kicked his gambling habit for good.

And he seemed to have done just that. Molly had never seen her brother looking so bright-eyed or *hopeful*. It was as if a heavy burden had been lifted from his strong, young shoulders. Was it the presence of a powerful male role model which had been the making of him?

In the very early days of her pregnancy, she'd persuaded Salvio that his London penthouse apartment was no place for a baby and he had surprised her by agreeing. So they'd moved into his sprawling Cotswold manor house where she had fun envisaging Marco and his siblings playing in those vast and beautiful gardens. Salvio had also bought this sea-view home in Naples where they tried to spend as much time as possible.

She sighed against the warmth of his skin. 'You make me so happy,' she whispered. 'I never thought I could feel this way.'

He stroked his fingers through her hair. 'It's because I love you, Molly. You're so easy to love.'

'And so are you. At least, you are *now*,' she added darkly.

He laughed. 'Was I such a terrible man before?'

'Terrible,' she agreed, mock-seriously. 'But terribly sexy too.'

'Are you angling for more sex, Signora De Gennaro?'

'There isn't time, darling. I've got to oversee last-minute preparations for tonight's dinner because there's a lot of pressure when you're cooking for your in-laws for the first time.' She frowned. 'And I'm worried I'm going to ruin the *capitone*.'

His fingertips tiptoed over her belly. 'You're not going anywhere until you tell me you love me.'

'I love you. I love you more than I ever thought possible. I love that you're a brilliant father and husband and brother-in-law and son. I love the fact that you've opened a football academy here in Naples and are giving a chance to poor boys with a dream in their hearts. How's that? Is that enough?'

'Curiously, it leaves me wanting more,' he growled. 'But then you always do.'

'More of wh-what?' she questioned unsteadily, as his hand moved towards her quivering thigh.

'More of this.' He smiled as he found her wet heat and stroked, enjoying her soft moan of pleasure.

'But, Salvio, there isn't time,' she said, her eyes growing smoky as he continued his feather-light teasing. 'What about the *capitone*?'

And then Salvio said something which, as a good Neapolitan, he had never imagined himself saying— but in the circumstances, perhaps was understandable. He pulled her on top of him and touched her parted lips with his own. 'Stuff the *capitone*,' he growled.

* * * * *

LET'S TALK

Romance

For exclusive extracts, competitions
and special offers, find us online:

f facebook.com/millsandboon

◎ @millsandboonuk

🐦 @millsandboon

Or get in touch on 0844 844 1351*

For all the latest titles coming soon,
visit millsandboon.co.uk/nextmonth